The L

OWAIN OWAIN (1929 – 1993) was a writer, physicist and language activist. He founded *Tafod y Ddraig*, the Welsh Language Society newspaper which remains a cornerstone of Welsh-language activism, as well as the ubiquitous 'dragon's tongue' logo. A prolific and eclectic writer, his biography *Mical* (1976) won Literature Wales's Book of the Year award. His novel *Y Dydd Olaf* (1976) published here in English translation as *The Last Day*. *Y Dydd Olaf* was the inspiration for musical artist Gwenno Saunders' 2014 album of the same name. Since then, it has been translated into Polish and Cornish, and was republished in Welsh in 2021.

EMYR WALLACE HUMPHREYS translates from Welsh and Portuguese to English, and from English to Welsh. A graduate of the MA programme in Translation Studies at University College London, he has had literary translations published in *The White Review*, *Your Impossible Voice* and *Joyland Magazine*. He was awarded a bursary to attend the Bristol Translates literary translation summer school and was a Visible Communities mentee for the National Centre for Writing. He was nominated for Deep Vellum's Best Literary Translations anthology 2024. An extract from this translation, with translator's introduction, was published in *New Welsh Reader* (Autumn 2023).

# The Last Day

Y Dydd Olaf

# Owain Owain

Translated by
Emyr Wallace Humphreys

Parthian || 2024

Parthian, Cardigan SA43 1ED
www.parthianbooks.com

First published in Welsh in 1976
© Estate of Owain Owain
Translation © Emyr W Humphreys, 2024
ISBN 978-1-914595-80-6

Editor: Gina Rathbone

Cover design, text design and typesetting,
Lyn Davies Design lyndaviesdesignfolio.com
Text set in Nexus Sans, Serif & Typewriter
Printed and bound by 4edge Limited, UK

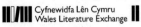 Cyfnewidfa Lên Cymru
Wales Literature Exchange

Published and translated with the support
of a Wales Literature Exchange translation
award through Arts Council of Wales National
Lottery Funding

Published with the financial support
of the Books Council of Wales

# The Last Day

## PROLOGUE : 01

WE ARE SURE the reader already knows the story of the final days of the previous century (then known as the 'Twentieth Century') and how they heralded the present age on Earth. Now, ten years after those events, we release the documents you have before you. They are as unusual as they are important, for there is no way to truly comprehend them; there is a scarcity of information on the Lost Century, and we have no other primary sources to bridge us, the people of the present century, to those of the last. The reasons for which should be obvious.

Two works are frequently mentioned in the main body of these documents: *Brave New World* and *Nineteen Eighty-Four*. If our interpretation of the few references made to these books is correct, then we may consider their loss one of the great tragedies of the Lost Century, especially in light of our efforts to establish its events.

The survival of these documents, compiled and bound anonymously, is nothing short of miraculous, and the rarest of gifts to us, believing as we do, the story behind their preservation. We have endeavoured to release them in the order they were found (we advise the reader to pay attention to the dates):

- Entries from the Last Diary of subject Marc;
- Miscellaneous documents from the final six months of the Twentieth Century;
- Entries from Marc's Early and Midlife Diaries;
- Miscellaneous correspondences from the mid century

All documents in this edition have been placed in chronological order. We, the Higher Committee of the New Few have not altered them in any way. However, for reasons that will become clear, we judged it wise to place the final entry of Marc's Last Diary in the second part of this prologue, keeping earlier entries from the same day in correct chronological order.

As previously mentioned, the original publisher of these documents remains anonymous. We also must disclose that they made three major alterations: firstly, by including a translation; secondly, by placing them in the order described above and dividing them into two parts; finally, by including these words at the end:

> *Marc:*
> *in praise and condemnation;*
> *forgiveness, persecution;*
> *for honour and derision.*
> *With love and hate I do this*
> *I knew; I never knew.*

## Final Diary Entry of Subject Marc

31/12/99 : PM

The Last Day: of this short century, my long life.

The Last Day, as there is no tomorrow – neither for me nor the residents of Lv.3. There's a tomorrow for someone. And on that tomorrow, the first day of the new century, the residents of Lv.4 will be the ones who receive their 'utmost honour'.

Yesterday was the end of an era for Lv.2 – that is, except for the hundred pairs of eyes glistening blindly in storage deep underground, the half-hundred pairs of testicles frozen solid somewhere else, and the thousands of tiny DNA cubes awaiting chemical resurrection in their plastic tombs even further below.

Our ex-hallmates on Lv.2 are now as still and lifeless as the sacks of pellets they feed us. Whose idea was it to sustain human lives with cattle feed? Tomorrow – but not my tomorrow – it'll be Lv.4's turn. The beginning of a century, the end of an era … for some reason, I'd rather go today than tomorrow. And if superstition is the reason for this twisted logic, then rejoice! For isn't this kernel of superstition deep inside my being proof of their failure to assimilate me completely?

I never imagined I'd be writing my final entry like this, though I'd known before coming that here at the Sunset House was where I'd be writing it. I knew I would *have* to … just not like this. They're very clever, I'll give Them that. Perhaps He is as well. Or should I say *that thing*? A clever oddity. By now I'm almost convinced that this really is the way, that I really am about to be granted the 'utmost honour' and fulfil my ultimate duty within the next three hours. Fratolish hiang perpetshki!

Yes, They are very clever, but that cleverness is how I got away with writing my diary like this. They're as cold as the storage basements, as lifeless as the residents of Lv.2 in the hereafter as of yesterday. Fratolish hiang perpetshki ...

I never did learn why They made us keep diaries. Nor why they're microfilmed and fed to the Computer-General. Something to do with social studies, I think. Discovering weaknesses in the system, the failures of Their assimilation regime.

Very clever, but not clever enough, because They forgot one little thing: the part of the Computer-General's translation programme that deals with sub-languages was deleted ages ago – and They don't know I know. The all-knowing Computer-General doesn't speak my little language! This diary will be digested by his electronic stomach without so much as a hiccup. He'll find nothing forbidden here because he doesn't understand a word of this trivial language, and everything, forbidden or not, will be microfilmed and safely stored in his electronic memory.

That's right: the whole diary as well as instructions on how to find the other documents, the letters and all, stored in the Final Diaries section, subsection: Unintelligible, sub-subsection: Semi-logical. Brilliant!

I'm lucky the electromagnetic messages from outer space, from $\Omega\Delta$, cause Them trouble, haunt Them. I'm lucky the Computer-General's competence is finite after all, as he strains under the weight of responding effectively to $\Omega\Delta$'s ambiguous messages, demanding the utmost from his computational programmes, those which replaced the sub-programmes that are now, according to Them, obsolete.

Those poor sods – a translation programme the Computer-General doesn't need anymore. It's the funniest thing! When will people – if that's what They are – be able to tell the difference between big and small, important and trivial?

Everything will be made available for the coming ages, if they ever come – if they haven't been cut short by Them. But for what purpose? If there are people left to read this diary, who will those readers be? Who will understand it? Treasure it?

It doesn't matter who. To me, right now, that's not what matters. Perhaps no one needs to read and understand it to find value in it. Isn't the making and the writing, what's important? Doesn't acceptance – or rejection – come later?

Only one thing has mattered to me over the last six months in the Sunset House: doing everything in my power (as little as that may be) to subvert the Great Untruth. For my own sake? Absolutely. For the sake of the world? Perhaps. I must keep the truth under wraps, protect it from their devices. The effectiveness of my means is not what's important. Complete success isn't either. What was – is – important is that I, a slave to my environment, have done and continue to do everything that can be done.

Six minutes left. Then comes the three hours of treatment. Three hours!

A whole tablespoonful of vinegar, says Joseff the barber from another lifetime, down the rooster's throat, three hours before the slaughter. You've never had better, tastier, more tender meat in all your life, no, myn diawl, he used to say, a lifetime ago.

Three hours and five minutes. Before the heavenly realms, the freezing stores and the unspoken hallways and basements …

Five minutes until the march. Like Lv.2 yesterday. Like Lv.4 tomorrow. And every other tomorrow for someone – there's no end to the arithmetic sequence.

Five minutes – now four – before They put an end to the little individuality left in this fleshy entity of mine. Four minutes before receiving the Council of Fraternity's 'utmost honour'.

Four short minutes. I have the right to sentimentality for some of these minutes. For what was. For Anna. For Mam and Aunt Bodo. For the hazy memory of my father. And for Siwsan (yeah, why not?). And even Pedr.

Three minutes. Why didn't they do a better job assimilating me? Why didn't any of them discover our little secret: our half-centimetre of platinum, our very own silver lining against the assimilation? They who are oh-so-clever?

Why am I leaving these fragments of tortured sentimentality? I could always just take out the platinum. It'd be easy; I could melt into the pattern, turn the soul into a sigh, the self into part of everyone. The eternal three hours in store for me would be acceptable then.

No – I've kept it in so far, so I'll keep it till the end. I will die a free man.

Two minutes. My name is Marc. I almost forgot to mention that. Seventy years and three weeks old. I was born seven decades ago. Before the assimilation. When you could see seagulls flying above the shore and hear the curlews crying out for rain. In The Winllan, where blackberries grew among the brambles and there were real leaves on the trees.

Before the assimilation? What assimilation? Isn't the assimilation as old as I am? As old as society? As old as the creation of Eve?

One minute – the gift of my last few breaths as a free man.

I'm appealing to you – yes, you! It's all here: programme number *five-three-seven*, sub-programme *two-three-five*. The Computer-General won't be able to read these forbidden digits in my little language – all his transistors would blow if he found out!

Please read what you've stumbled upon – I paid dearly for it. Use it. Bydd wych!

One minute. To Anna. To God.

# Part 1

**MARC'S EARLY DIARY**
*01/09/48 – 15/10/49*
Alongside miscellaneous correspondences
from the same period.

– interspersed with –

**MARC'S LAST DIARY**
*01/07/99 – 01/09/99*
Alongside miscellaneous documents
from the same period.

## *Marc's Early Diary* 1.

*01/09/48: evening*
September's begun. Next month I'll be at university.

Got a letter from Aunt Bodo. She wants to drop by before the month's out. Just finished wallpapering her kitchen, apparently. Pink and orange – blimey!

Mam's making blackberry jam. Pedr and I picked them in The Winllan yesterday. Got a chance to chat about university and the future. Both of us were lucky – full scholarships to study the same subject! Going to university together is going to be great for us, I reckon.

Went to the library, borrowed three books. An interesting novel called *Brave New World*. Also *Electronics: Alphabet of the Future*. Going to be useful, really visionary. Also, a book that gives a simple account of the war: *Theirs is the Glory*. That's one thing I like about books – they make the past and future part of the present.

Haven't seen Anna in town for days.

*Cont.: bedtime*
Saw Anna in town, just before tea. She was on her way home, just having tea with Rebeca. Had to go straight home, but was happy to walk with me to the end of the street.

Asked her if Pedr's story was true. She laughed and said she'd rather spend time with me than Pedr.

But she never did. I wonder why?

*Cont.*

Can't sleep. Sea is loud tonight, curlews louder. I remember Dad saying they cry out for rain around this time. He was always good at spotting omens.

House still full of blackberry jam smell. I can smell it from up here, even. Don't really feel like reading the new library books. Don't really feel like writing either.

Will try sleep again. Nos da, Anna!

# The Council of Fraternities

[Department of Health]

‹◊›

–« *fratolish hiang perpetshki* »–

### Voluntary Disclosure:

I hereby accept the invitation issued by **the Computer-General** to reside at the Sunset House for a period of six months from the date set out below, in order to ensure the necessary reduction of the general population.

I permit the relevant authorities, acting on instruction from **the Computer-General**, to make the most use possible of my assets once the period of six months has concluded, in order to aid in the completion of the objectives set out by **the Council of Fraternity**. To this end, I welcome all treatments during the subsequent six months considered to be for the enrichment of said assets on instruction from **the Computer-General**.

Signature  **Marc 35/278/29/516**
Date  1 September, 1999
Left shoulder serial code  100010100110

*fratolish hiang perpetshki*

17

# OFFICE PERSONNEL ONLY

| | |
|---|---|
| Welcoming date | 01/07/1999 |
| Date of storage | 31/12/1999 |
| Hall | B7/895/2068/L3 |
| Diary No. | L3/29/516 |

## RECORD OF TREATMENTS

| 1. | 2. | 3. | 4. | 5. | 6. |
|---|---|---|---|---|---|
| | | | | | |
| | | | | | |
| | | | | | |
| | | | | | |
| | | | | | |
| | | | | | |

## SUNSET HOUSE

left hand:          left leg:          right:

misc. organs:

DNA:          units.          remainders:          kg.

*30/09/48*

Went to buy more things for university today. Mam came with me to buy the suit. Got a nice one for a reasonable price from Siop y Bont. Then got a haircut at Joseff's. Old Joseff in good spirits – had the whole shop laughing. His banter's as sharp as his razors!

Planned to meet up with Pedr after lunch – no sign of him, as usual. Gone to The Twb, probably. Didn't feel like wasting time at The Twb with so much to do.

Aunt Bodo called by for a visit and to have tea with us. She was glad I was ready for university. Bright future and all that. She wanted to know all the details of the course, but clearly had trouble understanding the scientific terms. She's extraordinary, really – an old hand. Full of advice as usual, and she liked the suit.

After Aunt Bodo left, Mam said she'd asked if I'd 'carry her when the end comes'. What a thing to ask! I never thought someone with her views would care that much about what happens to bodies when they die.

Got a chance to read tonight. Finished *Brave New World* for the second time. Amazing – but also scary. Is it possible to fear something you don't believe in? I had two questions once I'd finished it again: if Huxley's prediction is correct, when will it happen? I probably won't see the day when human beings stop being human. And the second question: if he's incorrect, what kind of world will it be instead of the one described in the book? Impossible to answer.

Went through the cupboards before bed – stamps and cigarette cards and whatnot. Childish things which I'd stashed away. Thought about giving them to my cousin, but maybe I'll keep them a bit longer. It's hard letting them go, even if they're not very useful to me right now.

Saw Anna on the way back from town before tea, but she never saw me. At least, I'd like to think she didn't. Did she see me too, I wonder? Should I have gone after her? I'll write to her. The holiday will be over soon. Looking forward to the future. Just a few more days. It'll be here before I know it.

Think I'll be able to sleep tonight. Quite tired. Hope the curlews won't be too loud.

Nos da, Anna!

*Letter from Anna* 1.

02/10/48

Dear Marc,

Thank you so much for your letter – it came today. I wasn't expecting it, but am grateful to you for writing to me.

I didn't see you in the High Street the other day. I would have said hello if I'd seen you, of course. Why wouldn't I? I was at The Twb. It's a pity you weren't there. We had fun chatting and drinking too much coffee, as usual!

I'm sorry I can't meet you before you leave for university. Did you forget I'm still at school? *One* of us still has to go during the day!

Remember, Marc – it wasn't my choice to not come and see you.

All the best to you at university. You and Pedr are lucky to be going together. The Head mentioned you two in the school hall: the first time that two pupils from such a small school won full scholarships the same year, he said. His only complaint was that he didn't have the pleasure of sharing the future with you!

Perhaps I'll go to the same university as you next year. Dad's sent for a copy of the prospectus already, and he's hoping I get a scholarship like you two – to Dad all his geese are swans.

All the best to you over the border!

Very best wishes,

Anna.

02/10/48

Dearest nephew,

I cannot let you start your promising career at university without a letter from me, so I'm writing to you only a few days since that enjoyable afternoon – and delicious meal – with you and your mother.

I suppose I should impart some wisdom onto you, on behalf of your father, as it were. On the other hand, I'm not sure what gives me the right to pass advice on to someone who has earned an accolade in a field so alien to me, in an age that's becoming ever more incomprehensible; and to a generation which, quite frankly, scares me at times. (With a few exceptions, of course!)

But I think I should give you *one* piece of advice – nobody should ever give more than one piece of advice at a time, of course. What I tell you will probably stand you in good stead in all areas of life, at every moment, and for each generation experiencing such moments.

Choose your friends wisely. You know the saying: you can choose your friends, but you can't choose your family – so choose them wisely. Our friends are like our bookshelves – a truer reflection of ourselves, our character and personality, than anything else.

Make friends for your own sake – but choose those friends with great caution. I know you will never get to know someone completely, but at least try to get to know them well before sealing the friendship.

Now I've started preaching like this, I'm *itching* to say more.

But I must be true to what I said about *one* piece of advice at a time!

No – I must make an exception. And like every preacher who puts too much time into the first part of the sermon, I'll just skim over the rest: remember that today, not some time in the future, is life; and remember that everyone deserves respect, unless they demonstrate, through their attitude and actions, that they are not deserving of it.

That's all! Forgive me if this advice was unwanted; accept it, if you will, as one generation's attempt to impart some experience onto the next. We laid shaky foundations for your generation to build on. They're full of cracks, and all we can do is try and advise the new builders how to build something solid on them.

Poor you! I said I was scared of your generation – I wonder if it is just the pangs from my own conscience that are the cause of this fear?

I've just read what I wrote above. It's very different from what I'd intended writing to a young man on the threshold of a great adventure. But I will leave it as it is, just like Omar did.*

I have a favour to ask of you. I've already mentioned it to your mam, so perhaps she's told you by now.

As you know, I'm getting old. I've long since reached my golden years. When I was your age, the idea of dying was awful, and I thought (and dreaded) this fear would grow over the years. But it's not true; it wanes. Do you understand? The concept of dying, the necessity of death; as the later years pass by, it comes to be something pleasurable – no, not pleasurable … acceptable.

It's not that I want to die, but I know when the last days come, I'll be happy to go – perhaps even more than happy.

You know I follow Christ, and believe the grave does not mean the end. Yet the years rolling by have caused another change in

* Omar Khayyam (1048–1131) was a Persian mathematician, astronomer and poet, a collection of whose verses came out in Sir John Morris-Jones's translation in 1928 as *Pennillion Omar Khayyam*. This most likely refers to Khayyam's meditations on the nature of posterity and writing for the future.

me – the final deed, my final duties, are becoming ever more important. I cannot explain this, merely note the fact. But I wonder: do the living own death, and the dead own life?

Here's the favour: I would like to think of you as one of the four on the final journey. It would be easy for you to answer, just talk to your mam; we can discuss life and death as naturally as men discuss the weather, or football!

Dear Marc! What a letter to send you on an occasion such as this! I'd better be quiet now – my senility is beginning to show!

My very best wishes to you, Marc. Blessed be. And do what I did at your age – have a load of fun!

I attach a little present to help you with that!

God bless you, Marc.

Lots of love,
*Aunt Bodo.*

# OFFICIAL DOCUMENT: 02
01/07/99

## The Council of Fraternities
[Department of Health]

‹◊›

-« *fratolish hiang perpetshki* »-

| Birth statistics | 1-7-99 |
|---|---|
| Male | 5 Kilounits |
| Female | 7 Kilounits |
| No Sex | 7 Kilounits |

| RESERVES | |
|---|---|
| Organs | 100.37% of required |
| DNA | 100.26% of required |

| TERRITORIAL | |
|---|---|
| Planet A 72 | initial strategy ongoing |
| Planet A 71: | initial strategy complete |
| Planet A 70 | strategy phase 2 initiated |

#### OTHER

We rejoice in **the Computer-General**'s ongoing and successful interpretation of the electromagnetic messages sent from ΩA. New information in its entirety to be revealed in due course. Meanwhile let us praise **the Computer-General**'s ability in reacting in a fraternal manner to said interpretations.

*fratolish hiang perpetshki*

05/10/48

Off to university tomorrow! I can start living at last!!

Everything ready. Got new clothes, Mam's fixed the old clothes, and everything's carefully packed. Will buy the books when I get there; there's a second-hand bookshop next door to digs, I think. Even with the scholarship, I'll need to watch what I spend.

Went for a walk on the beach this afternoon, past The Winllan. Only a few leaves have changed colour. Didn't see many people along the way – just seagulls everywhere. No sight of Anna anywhere.

Called by Pedr's on the way back. He's ready for tomorrow. He's got the books already – brand-new ones. Arranged to meet him at the train station tomorrow. His mam's lovely – offered me to stay for tea. But had tea with Mam tonight – the last for a while. She was painfully patronising throughout the whole thing. And I got defensive and kept answering back more and more ungratefully, almost unwillingly. Poor Mam. It's a shame I didn't accept Pedr's mam's invitation to have tea over there.

Writing this – as usual – in the loft. Just had supper. Thought I'd have lots to say today of all days, but it's hard to know what to write about. Too much choice, from all the mundane details. But that's one good thing about keeping a diary – it makes you think about what's important, and what isn't.

Will most probably keep a diary because I want to write – and keeping a diary is the easiest way to do that. Also, it's a record – even though there's not much to record right now. It'll be better from tomorrow onwards – more events, and more important events to write about.

What will become of this diary, I wonder? I can imagine myself reading it at seventy years old in a comfy chair in the corner (if the paper survives over half a century!).

I wonder where? And who with?

I know who!

Have to answer Anna's letter before bedtime. Couldn't find her anywhere. Need to answer Aunt Bodo's as well.

Those two letters will be tricky to write. I know what I have to say to Anna, but not sure how to say it. And I have no idea what to say to Aunt Bodo – such a morbid letter! At least I'll thank her for the five-pound note. And (good idea!) I think I'll send her a postcard tomorrow, from the university – a colourful one. She does like her colours!

That's enough for today. Too much, perhaps. Again, didn't write everything I wanted to. It was like that all day – the desire and the result becoming separate, just like my mind and body. Almost forgot to write about this: I had a strange feeling of being 'different' to myself all day. Some sort of uncertainty: who am I? What am I? Why? And feeling myself suspended in a vacuum, between two worlds. I'd never felt like it before.

I hope Mam will be okay tomorrow and over the next few weeks. She'll be lonely once I've left, with the house loaded with the past. But I'm sure Pedr's mam will come and see her lots and 'compare notes' and keep each other's hopes alive. And I'm sure Aunt Bodo will come over quite often. Between Aunt Bodo and Pedr's mam, she'll have heaven and earth over for breakfast, lunch and tea! And supper too, if Aunt Bodo stays here overnight.

Will be sleeping somewhere else this time tomorrow. It's a strange feeling. Am sure everything will be fine. Why wouldn't it be? Looking forward to a new life – a new world! If I won the scholarship from a place like this, it'll be the world, next!

It's later than I thought. Better get some sleep. Will be tomorrow before I know it.

01/07/99: AM

They tell me to write, but They don't know I'm not one of The Rest – They don't know about the platinum.

So I'll write! I'll write boldly, like I'll never be caught red-handed; satisfied, like one who's discovered the imperfections within the perfect – and with the drive of one who knows his work will live on in the future.

We had a warm welcome this morning, perhaps some two hours ago. Two hours in the Sunset House, and here's me writing 'this morning' as if those few minutes already belong to the distant past.

There was never any hope of escaping. That's part of Their cleverness. I came here just like The Rest, with a smile on my face, seemingly of my own accord. But what choice did I have? The slightest sign of the assimilation's failure warrants a thorough investigation – then that'd be the end.

At least here there was the guarantee of another six months of life. There's the old saying, 'Where there's life there's hope'; if what I heard before coming here is true, then there's still hope that I can transmit some part of this truth for the ages.

Yes, it looks like what I heard about the diaries is true. Here's the proof, in front of me now. But what about the other rumour, that the programme for translating sub-languages is no longer part of the Computer-General's personality? I'll find out before long if that's true – tomorrow at the latest. If so, some truth will be kept in the Computer-General's memory, for the future. If not ... poor you, Marc!

If I had a glass of wine I would raise a toast to $\Omega\Delta$, whoever (or whatever) it is. A long and healthy life to you, $\Omega\Delta$! Keep at it, and long may you cause the Computer-General his indigestion!

So easy to assimilate us … Even to me, one of The Few who know of the platinum, the Computer-General is more man than machine. He has a personality and even suffers from indigestion!

More man than machine, turning mankind into machines …

Why is it we came here as false versions of well-rounded humans – of independent, sensitive, unique beings? Why the detailed planning, the complex, encyclopaedic sub-programmes, the elaborate assimilation systems? Is it just to create this image of freemen walking merrily through the gates of the Sunset House?

Who does this please? Is it Them? Or the Computer-General himself? To what end? Why do They need a false world full of free-willed human beings? Is it some echo of a primitive conscience which They once failed to assimilate? Or is it the Computer-General who demands this fake free world and people – in that case, why and what for? Is there a material, physical or electronic worth to a fantasy of this kind? Does the 'de-humaniser' himself need a false human world in order to guarantee the effectiveness of his plans?

I know we're in the Sunset House because of our 'resources'. I know the aim of the next six months is to enrich these 'resources'. I know we are raw material – to create life according to Their definition. If that's the case, I wonder if it's because sustaining life – of any kind, for reasons we cannot comprehend – is impossible without some sense of freedom? That's it: perhaps Their 'life' depends on our freedom, whether false or not.

But I don't really know. This, above all else, is the ultimate mystery.

Yes, we were warmly welcomed. Strange to think that even They still insist on using the symbolic act of the handshake. The feeling of Their skin was so unnatural. Human skin, once upon a time. It's likely The Rest, my platinum-less neighbours on Lv.3, never noticed how unnatural it felt.

Noticed? Does any 'noticing' happen among The Rest anymore?

Are their actions not just a series of conditioned reactions by now?

Of course, the unnatural skin of the hands which greeted us, the residents of Lv.3, didn't trigger any negative sensations or reactions in the others. There is no command in their assimilation programme that reads EVENT: TOUCH OF SKIN. REACTION: UNNATURAL SENSATION EVENT SYMPTOMS. They cannot react negatively to the touch.

The touch of skin on skin. This morning, to me, I felt a jolt in that touch. The jolt of fear, perhaps?

Twice – many years ago, before the present regime took power – did I experience such a thing. Once was with Mam. The last touch of my lips against her forehead. The jolt of fear? No, not fear. No emotion of any kind (though isn't the absence of all emotion itself an emotion?). Nothing. No reaction, no recognition. No nothing. That's why I felt such a jolt: just the utter, utter lack of reaction. Skin totally unaware of the touch of skin. No sensation. No empathy. No chill from the cold, either. Just empty, unfeeling distance. The disconnected isolation from that awful proximity. Touching without touch; so close, and the gulf in between so infinitely massive. And that profound jolt, the perfect negation of every jolt to ever come before – from my mother's first touch to her last moments of unknowing – electrifying the skin.

The other was the first time, with Anna at school. The perfection of first touch. A simple event: borrowing a book. Our fingers touching, perhaps by accident. Skin kissing skin in total innocence for a split second – the slightest moment. And that simple touch paralysing my whole body with a torturous, totally real, electrical jolt.

I knew my feelings for Anna back then. Did she know? Then, or any other time? It's hard to believe she didn't know. Hadn't that electricity been coursing through her body too? Hadn't our shared consciousness created it?

There was an echo – echoes – a handful of times afterwards. Each one different. The shock of discovering what I'd been imagining all the while – yes, her skin was pale and smooth and warm and alive. And the shock of discovering what I had never imagined: that the intertwining of bodies is not only a physical act.

How did you forget all this, Anna? Did you forget? And if you did, how can you explain – no, I'm rambling. Trespassing. This is not my task. What benefit to the future is there in these half-baked attempts at interpreting old experiences with partial and inaccurate information?

Control yourself, Marc – do what little there is to do in the time you have.

Very well. I'll write, not note; remember, not reminisce. This is all for you, unknown reader – I know nothing of your era, your race; and I cannot imagine your hopes and dreams.

Today, in the six months before the end of the twentieth century, the year of our Lord nineteen ninety-nine. Our Lord? Are you aware of our Lord in your time?

It's so difficult getting the truth onto the page! Where to start? What to explain? What secrets have we got which are commonly known in your time? And what obvious truths do we have which are total mysteries to you?

We live on a planet we call Earth. Is this something you knew? In the days of the Council of Fraternities – and the Computer-General – and Them. And The Rest, of course. And The Few – Pedr, myself and the few others who know the secret of the platinum.

Do you know of free will? You know more than I do if so! But really – like me, you must have at least some notion of what that means. Looks like it's forever lost on The Rest, but I'm not totally sure. It was wiped out, perhaps completely, by the assimilation. The assimilation way will finish the job.

And Them? It's difficult – even impossible – to say. They still have some free will, perhaps – sometimes. Lord only knows!

Only we – The Few – possess what I understand to be free will. There are a hundred of us, perhaps, on the face of the Earth. And there are times when the platinum loses its effect – when our thoughts wear the synthetic language of the Council of Fraternities, trespass on forbidden ground and attract the assimilation ray, full power, into our heads. It makes one go temporarily mad.

Remember this, as you read this diary: it's not always me who's writing. Sometimes it's obvious. Other times, you won't be able to tell.

Please! For your own sake, I must show you. I'm using the artificial syntax to think of the Computer-General – man-machine, the font of the Spirit of Fraternity, trying to understand the relationship – forbidden – still thinking in this synthetic language – my thoughts trespassing – the pain's starting – the ray – don't read – must write – don't fratolish hiang perpetshki

fratolish hiang perpetshki

fratolish of course Anna's different nobody but Anna knows Pedr doesn't know hiang perpetshki

fratolish  hiang only hope ΩΔ's messenger who are they? sabotages plans perpetshki

fratolish hiang perpetshki

fratolish the clock on campus says nine o'clock hurry Pedr Siwsan and Mari are coming where's Cwansa will you call for Cwansa give his wall a knock Pedr hey Cwansa give hiang perpetshki

fratolish hiang perpetshki

fratolish  hiang I can't refuse that Aunt just a little something I got five pounds from her once of course I will Aunt it's worth five pounds nearly said my pleasure to her lordy I best perpetshki

fratolish hiang perpetshki

fratolish  hiang perpet Mam Mam but she isn't answering if I knew why jam sandwich lovely tea Mam Mam is that her there of course who else but that's not Mam either yeah no yeah no shut your mouth and show some respect perpetshki

fratolish  hiang Anna Anna Anna pale and slender and slender and pale and no one but Anna knows what happened in the meeting perpetshki

fratolish Cwansa, he's black, his God's all black the Computer-General might be black to Cwansa the way hiang perpetshki

fratolish hiang perpetshki fratolish Siwsan Siwsan Siwsan Siwsan Siwsan Siwsan Siwsan Siwsan Siwsan hiang perpetshki

fratolish  hia they're making tasty blackberry jam full of tasty maggots with a tasty curlew with Lv.2 and Lv.4 and drinking coffee in The Twb but the Computer-General doesn't want blackberries nor maggots nor coffee he eats lives not loaves perpetshki

fratolish hiang perperperperperperperper

## Letter from Marc's Mother 1.

Dear son,

I am writing this before going to bed so I can post it when I'm in town tomorrow morning.

So, the first full day is over! I do hope you and Pedr got there safely yesterday, and that you're feeling a bit more settled today. No doubt you'll be finding everything unfamiliar and different, but I'm sure you will get used to your new world before long.

The house felt empty today. But Pedr's mam came after tea and stayed for an hour, just as we'd planned. We chatted about everything, but mostly you two, of course. Like how you both went together on your first day of school – and now to university.

We enjoyed our chat very much – telling all the old stories! Chatting about the future, too, and guessing what's in store for you two. And being thankful the War had ended before you grew up – the both of you are well aware of the horrors that took place.

Pedr's mam reminded me of the big argument you had at Anna's seventh birthday – who was going to marry her? And then I reminded her of the unforgettable duet you two had at the recital – your voice cracking, and Pedr practically tone deaf. Back then we didn't know how bright the future was to be for you two.

She wants to visit often, she says. I will be glad to have her company – we have so much to talk about. I gave her a jar of blackberry jam to take home, from the blackberries you two picked in The Winllan. She really appreciated it.

A letter came from Aunt Bodo today. (By the way, I do hope you sent her a letter when you arrived yesterday, to thank her for the gift and letter.) She's to call by next week to 'discuss some important matters', she says. I really want to ask her to stay the weekend – unless you were planning on coming home, of course. It would be a little change of scenery and would give me a chance to take a look at your clothes. They might need a couple of stitches here and there. Pedr's mam was also thinking you two might come for the weekend before long.

Will you let me know? Then (unless you were thinking of coming) I can let Bodo know she's welcome to stay. Her company would be such a blessing – she is so sound of thought, and I feel a sense of certainty after being in her company.

How are the digs? Are the rooms warm? How about the beds? It makes me so happy to know you are in good company. Do you need anything? Is the food okay? If you come home for the weekend, you'll be able to take something back with you – maybe cake or a pot of jam. And remember to bring your clothes for me to wash when you do come.

I'm looking forward very much to hearing all the stories.

Give my best wishes to Pedr.


God bless you, Marc.
Love, Mam.

*07/10/48*

Here at last!

This is the first time I'm writing since arriving. I have no idea where yesterday went – but it did go!

Starting from the start: the train journey was fine, had interesting company during the second half – two girls starting university as well, but reading the arts. They're called Mari and Siwsan. Mari reminded me of Anna, so spent more time chatting with Siwsan. Pedr has plans to meet them again – we'll see. Didn't see them again once we'd arrived, despite going to the welcome reception. Pedr was very disappointed.

Digs are great! Comfy room, right next door to Pedr. New and modern furniture, everything in good condition. Life is good. Slept quite well yesterday. Remember waking once – too dark to see anything – couldn't tell where I was, and couldn't understand at all why I couldn't hear the sea! Quite bizarre, as I don't hear it at home either, even though it's close by and quite noisy. Must have got used to it by now.

There's an African guy in the other room – I am between his room and Pedr's. He's in his second year, also reading Electrical Engineering, Physics and Mathematics. He's brilliant, from what I've heard. And like us, electronics is his main interest. His name is Cwansa, from West Africa. He reckons there's a bright future in electronics, and that applied electronics will be how we raise the standard of living for developing countries and restore freedom to the smaller nations.

Lectures haven't begun yet, just admin meetings. Feel quite

small in the halls, among everyone – but a giant here, in my own room!

We all want to go to the second reception tonight. Pedr's hoping Mari and Siwsan will be there. I'm sort of glad Cwansa's coming too. Not had the chance to write to Mam and Aunt Bodo yet. Will write before going to bed, unless it goes on too late. I think I'll write to Anna as well.

Got the chance to go to the second-hand bookshop next to the university, got lots of bargains. Pedr had bought new books before coming.

This should all be a lot of fun. The signs are all looking good. Really looking forward to the work – it will make a change from school, as I was getting bored of the work there. It'll be different here. Everything is so different here – almost like a new world.

I'm determined to do well. I had quite a bit of fun with work up to now. And if I was successful with things as they were before, then surely success will come with how they are now. The future is going to be an amazing challenge. I'm itching to face that challenge. There's so much to do – and I'll do it.

Somehow, I feel that life's finally begun – and I'm on the threshold of the future.

I wonder what Anna's doing now?

Pedr's knocking on the wall – we've designed a 'telegraph knock' already! My turn now to knock on Cwansa's wall.

The message: 'let's go!'

09/10/48

Dear Marc,

I was glad to get your letter this morning, though I was a bit confused when Dad told me – 'From Marc, I think!' How on earth did he know, I wonder?

Only a week has gone by since your last letter. Hard to believe it – but checked the date again, just to make sure. Your description of the train journey, the digs and meetings was really interesting – makes me keen to get this year over with quickly. I'll be going to university next year, by the looks of it; not sure which one yet, but your letter is helping me choose!

No sign of pretty girls in your description. I'm sure they're there somewhere! If so, Pedr will surely find them!

How's Pedr liking it? Are your rooms near each other? Pity he's not next door to Cwansa. How do you pronounce 'Cwansa', I wonder? I'd like to meet him, after reading your description of him.

No news from school – at least, none worth mentioning. Everyone much the same, but Rebeca and Ioan are quarrelling again. And to answer your question (even though I don't have to answer a question of the sort): no, I'm not 'going' with anyone. Why did you ask, I wonder?

I went for a walk towards The Winllan after tea. The leaves are fast losing their colour, but haven't turned yet. Not worth picking the blackberries anymore – they're hard and full of maggots. Picked a few wildflowers, but not many.

Saw Rebeca on the way back – without Ioan – and we went for a cup of coffee at The Twb. Having coffee there is great as ever.

Especially with Rebeca, without Ioan! Why did you never go? I never saw you there, at least. Pedr often went.

Rebeca told me the story of her fight with Ioan, after they'd gone to The Twb one evening with Pedr, a few days before he left for university. Ioan thought Rebeca was paying more attention to Pedr than to himself. Honestly, he must be very sensitive, because I didn't see anything out of the ordinary the half hour I was there – Pedr talking over everyone, as usual, and Rebeca, naturally, with no choice but to listen to him.

Dad's calling – wants me to make supper, probably. He thinks I'm doing homework at the moment – as far as I know!

Must go.

Thank you for the letter – I was glad of it.

All the best!

Kindest regards,
Anna.

P.S. Are you two coming home for the weekend, I wonder? A.

01/07/99: PM

The Sunset House. Day one. A day which, like us, is closer to the end than the beginning.

This is the end of the journey, the end of my journey. This is the mission I succeeded in accomplishing. Here is where the first step led. Was I that child? And this is the bright future. Was I that young man?

Yes – very bright future indeed. At a Sunset House.

It's surely a dream. This much is obvious. The whole thing is a dream. A hilarious dream, a nightmare of hilarity. Forgive the handwriting – I'm laughing!

Mam sewing my best pair of socks, placing them carefully in the suitcase so I arrive with warm feet; Aunt Bodo offering advice and sending a five-pound note so I arrive fresh after a boatload of fun along the way. Buying used books, saving the money to pay the fare for the train that terminates here.

The mathematician in me is number crunching: four meals a day, three hundred and sixty-five days a year, for the best part of the seventy years. If we take the years of scarcity into account, that's about a hundred thousand meals to prepare and eat. (Not to mention to source: growing, harvesting, processing.) One hundred thousand meals – just so this body could have the strength to get here, so its 'resources' can have a place of honour in Their storage basements.

The mathematician in me isn't clever enough to measure the other units that contributed to this success – the weight of disappointment, the rush of happiness, the strength of love and friendship, the coldness of unknowing. And all of it – the immeasurable whole – amounting to nothing.

No, that's not right. All that happened didn't happen just to get to this point. The happening was life, the purpose and justification of every action existing within the ends of the action itself. Life is not a sequence of chapters between a prologue and an epilogue, but a mosaic of events, with every event a full part of life unto itself.

To me, right now, writing this sentence is life.

But I'm tired. Thinking clearly is a struggle. I am 'old but this year born'.* And the treatments and drugs and conditioning are all leaving their mark. The platinum isn't a perfect defence; it'd be easy to slip back into the synthetic language and its soothing lullaby.

We were warmly welcomed this morning. Did I also write 'warmly' earlier? I don't remember – and They've taken those pages away.

I had a good idea of what was going on here before accepting Their 'invitation'. My old job made it easy to get a hold of some 'unofficial' information. Hard to believe yesterday I was in my old job! Is job really the right word for what I was doing? Why not! It's as good a word as any. And hasn't the Council of Fraternities since redefined every word? And besides, don't we redefine a word every time we use it?

Pedr still has his job. But he won't for long. A few more months, then he'll also reach the age of honour. A few more months – how could I ever forget Pedr's birthday?

Pedr's birthday! His tenner and my two quid left over from Aunt Bodo's fiver, Siwsan and Mari! Yes, we had a ton of fun. All blotted out by now, as far as I can tell. In hindsight, which was Aunt Bodo's most valuable contribution, I wonder: the advice, or the money?

Poor, dear, fickle old Pedr. Like me, lucky enough to make it as one of The Few. Lucky? Yes. If you can call a free man with no freedom

---

\*   From the ninth-century anoymous poem *Henaint* (Old Age), (*Welsh Poetry Music and Meters*, tr. Howard Huws, Gwasg Carreg Gwalch, 2017): This leaf, by the wind blown – along,/Woe to it fate's turn!/Now old, but this year born. (Y ddeilen hon, neus cynired – gwynt/ Gwae hi o'i thynged! Hi hen, eleni ganed.)

luckier than a malleable puppet in another's hands. The Rest are puppets, of course. And Them too, most likely. Puppets in the hands of the Computer-General, creating fake life.

Why all this faking? What's the reason for these plastic flowers bordering plastic lawns? And the warm welcome this morning? If we're merely puppets, then what's the point of all this? Would the Computer-General – and Them too – be all the poorer for overlooking something?

Everything's obscure. And the questions keep gathering.

Why is the Computer-General so determined to guarantee the survival of these machines in the form of humans? What are flesh and bone and imperfect organs to him? Why the cavernous stores of chemicalised life – from the material qualities of life itself – in the storage basements?

And why The Rest? They aren't the means for the continuation of life anymore, but merely means for replenishing the materials of life.

A world of machines in flesh; fleshy extensions of the metallic body and electronic soul of the Computer-General. They play at being eating, breathing and walking human beings who love, grieve, work the land, and are totally sterile.

I feel sick to my stomach. Perhaps it's the treatments, and the drugs. Or the Computer-General's interpretation work.

Six months. Here. Lord – let me rest in peace!

I've only seen the Computer-General as Man once. He looked beautiful. And as Machine: no one except Pedr knows I've seen it. I never touched it.

The spirit of Fraternity is with us always.

'Fratolish hiang perpetshki.'

I, Marc, wrote this. I, one of The Few.

*Letter from Pedr* 1.

My dear friend,

I'm sure you'll get this in time. Thankfully, there are ways to communicate with people who understand.

I know you're on your way to the Sunset House today. What can I say? What can I do? There's no hope, Marc. It's too late – for you and me and every one of us. I see no hope.

Why write at all? I can't not. There's something heartening about being hopeless together!

I worry, Marc. It gets unbearable at times. Remembering what you could have done. How long ago, I wonder? Do you remember that meeting – what, fifteen years ago? Was it too late then? Was it too late in those first directionless little meetings – a lifetime ago?

There's still a way for us, The Few: take out the platinum. You know how. It's easy. Then the seamless assimilation and great contentment.

It's one way.

But maybe things aren't totally hopeless. Something's happening with $\Omega\Delta$, on a larger scale than before. I'm not sure what, but it's important. The CG is at full capacity – and the messages haven't been completely interpreted. I believe more and more inferior programmes are being transferred to the $\Omega\Delta$ interpretation programme and the system's starting to get weaker. Is there still hope?

Do you remember (over half a century ago!) that first journey down to university on the train? Ah, the train! We didn't half have a laugh with Mari and Siwsan (especially Siwsan)!

I have to tell you this Marc, then I'll leave it. If there's one thing that's still important, it's this: it was my fault; mine and Cwansa's, not Anna's. You must believe this, because it's the truth. I don't need to explain further. It's enough just to try and tell you the truth. It was not Anna's fault.

Marc, my dear friend – having said this, what else is there left to say? I'd tell you if I knew.

Is there anything after this, Marc?

I don't know when to stop writing, nor how.

We had fun, didn't we – and why not? Those were the days! I'll treasure them. So much fun.

Let me know – somehow – if anything happens. There may still be hope.

Remember the fun! And the train! And $\Omega\Delta$!


Dal ati, Marc!
· Pedr.

## Marc's Last Diary : 03

01/07/99: Evening

The end of the first day – the first of the last days. Perhaps.

What did I write this afternoon? Impossible to remember. And They've taken the pages away from me, just like this morning. I remember writing something about Pedr. And Anna, most likely. It's hard to remember. Was it even me who was writing?

It's inexplicable, our need to keep diaries. Except here – there's no choice here. But why do we do it voluntarily? Who for? If for ourselves, then how to explain the instinctive temptation we have to change the odd word or erase the odd sentence in old diaries? We cannot fool ourselves like this.

I've been tempted, more than once, to do this: change something small, here and there. But I never did.

Except once. I changed a sentence in an old diary – a laughably weak attempt to make the past easier to live in, and the present easier to explain. What if we could change the event and not the sentence? Poor us – the present is apparently harder to explain now than ever before!

I wonder if it's not for ourselves we keep diaries? So big-headed! What would the value of this little narcissistic self-portrait of mine be to one of my descendants? Witness me! What would anyone gain by reading the obscure life and times of one of their forebears?

No, I never kept my diaries for others. I kept them for myself. A weak, mad attempt to slow the passage of time, to freeze it in place, to curb the wild stampede.

And what's more, I got to prove to myself that it all wasn't fake – real black letters on white paper shouting: 'It's true! It happened! It is! You are!' Creating an island of solid land for a word to take refuge, when there's nothing but sea around it. Somewhere to escape to, where there's none of the uncertainty of tomorrow, nor the unreality of today.

There's also another reason: how the old man gets to read the early chronicle of a young man so full of hope, ending up reminiscing in the corner with a smile on his face – 'from this acorn the oak tree grew'. Yes, this oak tree, full of oak apples, hard and bitter, with maggots in its crooks. An oak tree which has no acorns.

Getting Pedr's letter was nothing short of a miracle. Getting it here, of all places. Is that not in and of itself a sign of hope?

Poor Pedr, reminding me of the platinum! As if I could ever forget about it! If ever there were a literal meaning to the term 'silver lining', it's the platinum. Beneath it is where the soul dies. Without it, without the half-centimetre of refuge, I am nothing but a supply of organs, DNA and cattle fodder, waiting until the time is ripe before disappearing (receiving my 'honour') into the freezing stores below.

Pedr, Pedr ... You don't think that I, Marc, am ready to take out the platinum, do you? And murder my own soul? I thought you knew me better than that, after all these long years.

Pitiful Pedr, do you still think that silly little episode between you, me and Anna still matters? Today, with the world living through its nightmare, and life becoming death itself – do you still think that going over that silly old episode would be anything other than the shameful echo of the misvalues and false impulses of our miserable, greedy little past lives?

And Pedr, Pedr, the most pathetic of men – is it not you, one of The Few, and your living, free soul – who is asking this of me?

The bell. Last treatment of the day. Then these pages will be collected. They don't waste time here.

I thought I heard a curlew crying out – I must be getting senile! Where are they nesting now – if they really are? And the seagulls that used to whirl overhead in The Winllan? Are there still seagulls? And The Winllan? And the sea? And ripe blackberries? Or ones full of maggots, even – live, free maggots, unruly, gleefully so, squirming blissfully free. Or dry blackberries, full of seeds, the end of October, rich in promise.

Second bell. Must stop.

End of the first day; the first of the last.

# The Council of Fraternities

[Department of Health]

‹◊›

-« *Fratolish hiang perpetshki* »-

### Daily Report: Sunseteer, Individual

| Period | Day 1; Month 1 |
|---|---|
| Hall | B7 / 895 / 2068 / L3 |
| Name | Marc 35 / 278 / 29 / 516 |

| Treatment 1 | successful |
|---|---|
| DNA | 100.26% of required |

**DIARY**

| Length | 3,7 units |
|---|---|
| Status | indecipherable |
| Forbidden Content | n / a |
| Storage | A32689 / X3 / B7 |

*fratolish hiang perpetshki*

## Letter from Siwsan 1.

Dearest Marc (The Monkey!),

You went home, didn't you, kiddo? To Mam Bach and Anna Banana? Well, I hope you had fun. Is she fond of bananas? Anna, not your Mam Bach. You forgot about Saturday, didn't you? Perhaps the grass is greener at home. I had fun too, so it makes no difference... monkey!

When will I see you again – or will Pedr have to do? He and Mari had a heck of a row on Saturday. The grass is drying up on that side, I reckon.

I don't trust Cwansa. Don't get him to take your place if you're not up for hanging out anymore. I grew up with stories about people like that ...!

Must finish an essay now. Hate the work already. Won't be here after this year, sure enough! Can you afford a maid? Let me know (about tonight, not next year, monkey!)

Siwsan.

P.S. What's that crazy idea of Cwansa's? The 'Society of Fraternity' or something silly like that. You can tell me all about it tonight – hee-hee! Hurry, monkey, there's no life in a world of essays.

Mari's just called by. She's back with Pedr. You know what they say about old flames. How about a double date?

01/11/48

Glad to be back at digs. Didn't enjoy spending the weekend back home. I wonder why? Is just a month long enough to undo the effects of eighteen years? It's hard to believe that – but still, it seems like it.

It's so different here. I'm myself here. But back home I'm a part of everyone – a part of Mam, Aunt Bodo, of this, that and the other. I suppose a part of everyone – that is, everyone except Anna.

I don't understand Anna. The few hours I spent with her didn't bring any new sense of recognition – a new understanding.

She ran back, all the way from The Winllan to town – well, walked quickly, at arm's length. And talking as quickly as she was walking, about everything, Pedr and co. – without looking at me.

I'm not sure what's the use of keeping such a boring diary. Only things that would be forgotten otherwise should be recorded – but some things are better left forgotten, so why keep them alive?

Anna doesn't understand me. She doesn't understand how important she is to me. Unlike Pedr. Anna's just a girl to Pedr. A bit of skirt like Mari. Or Siwsan, no doubt – knowing Pedr. I wonder if Pedr slept with Siwsan in the few days I was away? Probably.

Is Anna telling Pedr about me? They're all the same; the only topic of conversation Siwsan has is the other boys she's been with – and all the details. What if I were to start talking about Siwsan to Anna? What would Anna think then?

I dare not mention Siwsan to Anna. But honestly, I talk about Anna to Siwsan. Maybe it's a sort of payback. Once I called Siwsan

Anna – she didn't even notice. But I wouldn't fancy Anna calling me Pedr – mistake or not.

I think I understand Siwsan. And understanding Siwsan is key to understanding Pedr as well. Perhaps Siwsan to me is like what Anna is (and what Mari and the rest are) to Pedr.

Maybe that's why I'm so glad to be back here. Siwsan's here – and I get her. I get her because I don't have to get her – just accept her. So different to Anna; Anna knows but doesn't acknowledge it, and that drives me mad.

The company in The Twb was completely infantile. Gulping down tasteless coffee, vainly blowing smoke and chatting nonsense. Alright for Rebeca and Ioan. But Anna doesn't belong there. Nor do I.

Why was it so important that we left The Winllan for The Twb so quickly? And for goodness sake: why so awfully close at The Twb – pushing her chair closer to mine, drinking from my cup – after fleeing back to town?

I'm glad to be back. And thankful for Siwsan's honesty. There's a kind of perfect consistency (as well as 'morality') to Siwsan: her 'no' in The Winllan is a 'no' in the café, and every 'yes' in the café is a 'yes' in The Winllan.

I'm fond of Siwsan (fond? it's hard to find the right word). Fonder of Siwsan than of Anna. But I love Anna.

Love? What is love? Whatever it is, that's what sparks that odd jolt I feel when I touch Anna's hand – more striking than Siwsan's subtle touches. Who said that bodies are only made of flesh?

This academic work wasn't what I expected it to be a month ago. It's interesting, and easy enough, but too much like schoolwork. Many of the lecturers are just schoolteachers – less chalk dust on their clothes, perhaps. One of the lecturers is nothing more than a human gramophone; Lord save us – a man in the form of a machine! Did I work so hard for this?

Mam wasn't much better. Sewing socks and packing a pot of blackberry jam wrapped in layers of grey paper. Was that why I went back home? And why didn't she want Anna to come over for tea on Sunday? Maybe I'll bring Siwsan along next time, for the hell of it. I'll introduce her to Anna too!

Pedr's mam blamed me more than Pedr for him not coming home for the weekend! Why, damn it, did Mam invite her over for tea on Sunday afternoon? Saw Anna's precious father too. Who does he think he is? And who does he think Anna is?

Lecture time – with the human gramophone. Pedr's knocking on the wall: 'time to go!'

Didn't even know he was in.

08/07/99

A week in the Sunset House. That's how we acclimatise – to everything. And of course, the little of the assimilation ray that makes its way into the brain, past the platinum, makes the acclimatisation that much easier.

Without a doubt, the electromagnetic messages from $\Omega\Delta$ are having a massive effect on the Computer-General. They don't ask me to keep diaries every day – there's been a week's gap since the last one; but I was made to understand (via my 'contacts') how important it was that residents kept daily diaries – indeed, for a reason that's beyond me, it's one of the factors that ensures the success of the Council of Fraternities. It's obvious that part of the sub-programme for the diaries has been transferred to help with interpreting $\Omega\Delta$'s messages. Keep at it, $\Omega\Delta$!

What on earth do The Rest write in their diaries? If it's just the shibboleths, what use are they to the Computer-General? What value is there in page after page of fratolish hiang perpetshki, with the odd formula here and there for variety?

How will the repetition of these shibboleths guarantee the success of the Computer-General? Does it somehow create healthier organs, richer glands, and a better supply of DNA in the writer? Is a sort of psychosomatic effect the explanation? Because – if I understand correctly – the main purpose of the six months in the Sunset House is the 'enrichment of resources'. That, plus the diaries, and (according to the form) the need to 'ensure the necessary reduction of the general population'.

We – or at least The Rest – are the 'general population'. I suppose They are the 'locals', then! But what about The Rest and their diaries? What could be in them but shibboleths and replication? Mechanical descriptions from conditioned reactions to a synthetic world. Take 'I saw a green and yellow leaf falling on the ground' as an example. I saw = a permitted description of the reactions of optic nerves to a light stimulus. A green and yellow leaf = made of plastic, but growing and yellowing and falling to the ground. Such is the environmental sub-programme's cleverness. And that literary pearl – the similar pearls – conceived from one of the sub-programmes of the Computer-General himself! It's an unbelievable state, totally inexplicable, the meaning and value of these computational complexities which are beyond my imagination, let alone my knowledge.

Do They keep diaries full of shibboleths, I wonder? If They do, then there's a chance They recognise that they are shibboleths. Do They understand that the green and yellow leaf is made of plastic? It's difficult to know to what extent they've been conditioned. And how many of Them there are. Are They dead? Or – is that the reason for the storage basements full of 'resources'? To what extent do they depend on the Computer-General? And he on Them? Is the Computer-General – the Man – one of Them?

Funny to think that Pedr and I could have been one of Them. Why didn't Pedr agree, I wonder? Pedr of all people! And on the other hand, wasn't Cwansa's agreeing to join equally inexplicable?

And Anna. How, how, *how*? But I don't think this is the truth. Anna? Her warm skin now cool and metallic? Her strong will now turned weak? If that's true, then that's not Anna, and it never was. The real Anna stopped being Anna years before this. I wonder when? Before the last meeting? Before the first meetings? As long ago as the campus lawn? Or The Winllan, even?

Was she ever the real Anna?

What happened in that last meeting, fifteen years ago, before the Council of Fraternities properly took over? Pedr's last letter wasn't very reassuring. He didn't cast any new light on Anna. 'It was my fault.

Mine and Cwansa's, not Anna's.' Was Pedr talking about the last meeting before the Council, or something else, so very unimportant?

The last meeting was fifteen years ago. In 1984 hiang perpetshki

fratolish hiang perpetshki

fratolish hiang perpetshki

Ubi-kiang hiang perpetshki

Ete-kiang hiang perpetshki

Homni-kiang hiang perpetshki

Al computerex

Al computerex

Al computerex there isn't no there isn't there isn't no nor no one no not twinkle twinkle little star how I wonder what you are gee ceffyl bach yn cario ni'n 2 here we go gathering nuts in May and on that farm he had a cow with a moo moo here and a want mam so mam so mam so mam-mam-mam da-da-da-da

## Marc's Last Diary : 05

09/07/99: PM

Something happened yesterday – with the diary. But I'm not exactly sure what happened. I suffered the worst pain I've ever had in my life. It's very likely that I thought – in the synthetic language – of a highly forbidden topic.

But what was it? Had I tried interpreting the nature of the Computational Trinity using the synthetic language? It's very high on the list of forbidden topics, and thinking of it in any form will trigger an overwhelming blast of the assimilation ray into the errant mind.

Or I wonder if I'd thought of the year nineteen eighty-four? That's one of the most forbidden topics for two reasons.

The Computational Trinity – the Computer-General as Machine, as Man, and the Holy Ghost, the Spirit of Fraternity. Is this an intentional attempt to metaphorize the old? Aren't the mysteries the same? Is not the same relationship between the unity's various aspects the ultimate mystery of the present order, just like the old one? Isn't the emphasis They put on the importance of acceptance of – instead of interpreting and understanding – the nature of the interrelationship proof that a religion of some kind plays an unignorable part of every order, no matter how 'logical' that order?

And the other forbidden topic – nineteen eighty-four. That was the year the Council of Fraternities came to power, of course. They aren't very willing for that era to be discussed. And before the Council was properly established, there was the book of the same name as the year which described the order of things too closely for it to be considered an acceptable book.

I know, through sheer experience, which topics are forbidden. But even so, I err at times and think about them in the synthetic language of the Council of Fraternities, despite the consequences – the torturous pain – that come of that.

Why do this? Doesn't it prove the strength and force of the original conditioning that was worked on us during the 'innocent' years before the rise of the Council of Fraternities? Before direct assimilation? I didn't realise back then how strong its effects were; yet still, that 'simple' conditioning is what brought us to the present state.

I hope my slip up wasn't noted yesterday, in one of Their machines; there's a thought interpreter of some sort in this 'room', of course. Or worse – if 'nineteen eighty-four' was my crime, had I written it in numerical symbols instead of in words, then the Computer-General would understand the forbidden symbols! If that's the case – poor you, Marc!

But that was yesterday, and it's already today. Maybe nothing will come of it. Perhaps ΩΔ, once again, is stealing sub-programmes.

I hope nothing comes of it. Not just for myself, but for every one of The Few.

Dear Pedr – forgive me my mistakes. Don't we all make mistakes?

Anna too – if it's true. No, it can't be! Anna isn't one of Them. The idea is beyond all imagination. I want to see her.

But what if she was one of Them? Even so – I'd still want to see her, but from afar. Too far to touch her. Too far to touch the skin that was once smooth and pale and warm; and too far for her to see me.

I wouldn't want her to see me as an old man, seventy years of age. And her as one of Them, still young and full of grace. Young and full of grace, and her skin metallic and cold. Would she look – from afar – like the Anna that sat on the campus lawn, an age ago?

And who, I wonder, does that borrowed youth belong to? From which basement did they dig out that expensive grace? Life is a never-ending irony. Is it not possible that Anna's deathless new body might be made up from Siwsan's pure and simple body?

09/07/99: Evening

Today, for the first time ever, I saw one of the unhuman abominations. Oh Lord, why have you forsaken us? What have we done that you have forgotten us? Why couldn't I have died before this?

I know of their existence. There were rumours amongst us, The Few, for years; rumours boastfully confirmed by Them.

I saw him (him?) through my window, in the metallic sunshine. Lord, why did you not extinguish the sun before shining down upon this new Adam?

He was a young man (man?) – if his appearance is anything to go by. One of the very first ones, most likely – one of the few created from the early failed experiments. The fruits of the latest experiments haven't left the Maternal Lab yet, despite metabolic processes having doubled in speed.

He was walking – if walking is the word – across the plastic lawn, towards the imitation stone wall. He walked (or at least moved) across the lawn until he reached the wall. Then he turned ninety degrees and headed along the far wall, and through the doorway.

I saw him shaking his head along the journey, to the rhythm of a heartbeat. From left to right, right to left.

My Lord, my Lord, why have you forsaken me?

He wasn't black nor Asian. Yes, They're very clever: they made him white instead. Then after fleeing through the doorway, I saw you, Anna, standing on the lawn. You were smiling. I only imagined you, of course. Pure imagination. Oh Anna, did it all come to this?

The smell of straw bales came through the window – it came from

Them; one of the sub-programmes created it. But along with the straw smell came the light fragrance of your body and your hair, from years ago. That smell is mine and only mine – not Theirs.

It's mine, at seventy years of age, a decrepit old man looking through a window one September, spotting a young woman on the green lawn, and filling his body with the fragrance of hers, and living out his youth within hers.

I'm smiling. Now I'm laughing. I'm laughing so much the noise is flooding out of this luxurious prison cell. I'm laughing – wildly, wildly, wildly! What else can I do except laugh? I'm laughing as I get to live to see the son of Man crossing the lawn under God's sunshine, and see Anna standing there, on the lawn one September.

I stand by the following depiction: see here, oh Computer-General, an animal which possesses the gift of laughter!

17/06/49

Dear Marc,

You will be on your way home from university by the time you get this. This is why I'm writing to you: I want you to know my feelings before I see you here – if we see each other again.

I didn't want to write to you ever again after what happened last time you and Pedr were here. It wasn't the first time either. I thought, once, that we were beginning to understand each other; but it's obvious to me, after the last time, that there's no longer any hope that'll ever happen.

You don't understand me, Marc. Either that or maybe you thought I was someone else last time you came.

It's your business, of course, what you do away from home. That has nothing to do with me. But when we were all at The Twb, it was obvious, according to Pedr, that Siwsan (whoever she is) wasn't just his friend.

I wonder if you thought I was that Siwsan? If she means something to you, then why are you so keen to be with me? Something to tide you over until you go back to university? Do you think that's an okay thing to do? And something I'd be happy with?

It's better we don't see each other again. It's obvious you don't want to accept me for who I am – and I cannot be anything else. Not even to you.

I'm sorry, Marc. I thought things would have worked out differently. Please don't reply to this. For one thing – there's no answer to be had. And another thing – Dad's not very happy that I'm getting so many letters from you.

I'm going away for the summer holidays, as you know. And we'll quite possibly be further away from each other than ever. It's probably for the best. It would be dangerous for us two to be in the same place away from home.

Kind regards,
   Anna.

*09/07/49*

The first year of university has flown by. Looking back, it dragged at times – but the time went somewhere.

What was the long and short of it? Shame I didn't keep a daily diary, as it would be easier to answer that question then. But I never did – there's been a ten-month gap.

Ten months: the blank diary has answered the question after all!

It's nice to be home. I was starting to get bored of university. Pedr as wishy-washy as ever, and with Cwansa, there seems to be some bitterness bubbling beneath the surface. Siwsan's morals are less moral than ever, scaring me with how naturally she follows her unconventional lifestyle. If ever there was a champion of loving without love, it would be Siwsan.

Haven't seen Anna again since coming here. And remembering her last letter to me, that doesn't surprise me. It's obvious she's avoiding me – or at least she's not trying to meet up with me.

I'd like to see her one of these days. On her own terms. Why does just touching her hand give me more of a jolt than burning my whole body in Siwsan's fires?

Siwsan and Anna. What makes Siwsan Siwsan, and Anna Anna? To what extent is Siwsan – and Anna in the same way – to be praised for her excesses, and condemned for her failures? Does Siwsan create Siwsan, and Anna create Anna? Or are they, like each other, isolated beings? And to what extent do they, through me, create each other?

Do I create them? Am I making Siwsan be what she is – and Anna not be what she is?

It's an unsettling idea – that I'm living not only my own life, but Siwsan and Anna's as well. And those two living a part of my life – they and Mam and Aunt Bodo and Pedr and Cwansa – yeah, and even Rebeca and Ioan, and Mair – even Anna's dad and Pedr's mam, and the human gramophone and Joseff the barber – all living a part of my life for me.

I am what they are; they are what I am. Love thy neighbour as thyself – the neighbour is you.

Went for a walk in The Winllan this morning. Just me. Didn't want anyone's company – not Pedr not Anna nor anyone else. But maybe my Dad's. I would love it if my Dad were still alive. I would have loved his company, walking towards The Winllan, through The Winllan and towards the beach.

I think about him every time I hear a curlew crying out, and every time I see one of the seagulls flying above the shore, and every time I look at the miracle of the trees in The Winllan.

I only have a hazy memory of him, and that memory, somehow or other, is attached to the curlews and the seagulls and the trees that grow in The Winllan. I wonder if we'd ever gone for a walk, us two, way before even memory began, hand in hand, towards The Winllan? Was that the first time I learned there was a big round world around us?

Maybe that's why I would love his company again. Would I discover, once again, that there's a big round world around me?

His company first. Then I think Siwsan – not Anna – would be my second choice, right now. What things – what qualities – bring those two together? Is Siwsan's secret what I believed was my Dad's secret too? Two people totally aware of the big round world around them?

On the way back through town, I saw a nightmare. A girl – ten years old? – holding her father's hand. Poor thing! There is no God. At least, not Mam and Aunt Bodo's God. That God and this little girl couldn't coexist in the same universe.

Poor little thing! Who created her, I wonder? Her walk wasn't a walk. Nor was her face a face. Why? And who? Was mankind guilty of creating this yellow-haired monstrosity? Was mankind guilty of creating the *possibility* of the existence of this yellow-haired monstrosity?

## Letter from Aunt Bodo 2.

My dear nephew,

It's been almost a year since my last letter to you. And although we've seen each other more than once in the meantime, I feel this letter will be more closely related to my previous letter than our meetings in person.

I wonder – is this proof that the world of paper and ink is different to the world of personal and physical touch? Not just the medium is different, but 'you' and 'I' are as well. Some things are easier to say on paper than on the tongue – the opposite is true for other things. Is simple shyness the reason for one and ineptitude for writing the other? Or is it more complicated than that – that we also live in a world of 'paper and ink' which is different from the world of faces and voices? And the two worlds, although connected, are separate?

There I go, philosophising again! And this letter was meant to be very simple. But there it is – almost a year since my last letter.

The simple message is to invite myself over for tea – and stay a few days. You can ask your mam which day works and let me know.

By the way – don't spend your money on a colourful postcard as usual. A short letter would be just fine! I prefer seeing the town in its rich grey tones than looking at a false picture of it, all garish and without significant shading.

Almost slipped back into philosophising again!

The money you save by not getting a coloured postcard should allow you to buy more ink than usual. And, as it is your holidays, you won't need to – in your words – 'rush to catch the post'!

And remembering the theme at the beginning of the letter, you won't end it so quickly 'as we'll have a chat about everything soon'! You knew we wouldn't be talking about many things that could have been discussed in a letter!

I'm itching to know (on paper, not in person) how the first year at university went. I know we talk plenty face to face – about the year, and the colourful postcard from the hostel at the start of the year. But I never got to learn about your 'paper and ink' world so far!

Yes, I'm nosy. But if I needed justification, then I would plead 'your father's sister'. But there doesn't need to be a justification, does there? Your business is my business. Part of your success belongs to me; and if failure comes (most likely it will come – it comes for everyone), a part of that, too, belongs to me.

You've made friends, of course. You told me about one or two of them – nice polite boys from what you told me. What about a 'paper and ink' description of them? And tell me about your other friends – the two (or is it three) girls? I also was young, once!

Must finish to catch the post! But of course your Aunt Bodo has to offer some advice! 'Paper and ink' advice – the kind that doesn't roll off the tongue in a chat: you're making new friends – of both sexes. Well done. Your horizons are broadening, and the feelings are deepening. That's how it should be. But with this, the possibilities multiply, the actions become more complicated and their consequences more fateful.

Remember: no voluntary action – from the body nor mind – ends in and of itself. It lasts forever. You cannot put a full stop after it. You can forget all about it; but it lasts until the distant future.

That's why I told you once that today is life. Today is tomorrow. The continuation of your today is your tomorrow.

Make the most of your today, Marc!

Sending this letter soon – before the complementary conversation!

Send my kindest regards to your mam – and let me know about coming down for tea.

Kindest regards,
    Aunt Bodo.

10/07/49

My dear Monkey,

You didn't have to take our agreement literally, did you? 'Loving without love' doesn't mean not writing anymore, now does it?

Anyway, I got a hold of your home address – as you can see! A prize if you can guess who gave it to me!

Do you miss me, my pretty Monkey? I miss you. Ah, don't worry! Admitting that you miss me doesn't mean you love me, and it doesn't lead to (forgive the next word) marriage. But maybe it's not missing – the same way someone hungry doesn't miss a loaf of bread.

How are things over there? Is Anna a little less uptight? You should have more fun after everything I've taught you – silly monkey! Tell Pedr I say hi.

Not too sure what I'll do next year. We'll see. Or should I say I'll see? But that's not why I'm writing to you. It's something more serious (I'm such a hypocrite!). I had a long chat with Cwansa – just a chat, Monkey! As you know, he went home the day after you did, same as me. Things are going great at the Council of Fraternities, and Cwansa's on fire wanting to spread the message. There are three branches now, about sixty members. There are also three minority movements that are interested in forming an alliance. Believe you me – Cwansa's started something!

You should have heard it! I'd never seen him so sure in his vision. He said some very cutting things: 'Our minority is more fortunate than your minority. We cannot disown nor hide the colour of our skin. That's why we aren't a schizophrenic minority.

And that's why we don't have to prove to our own people that we're different.'

Cwansa's totally convinced that the Council of Fraternities has a global future, and he wants to bring the alliance together for the first time, the middle of next month. You can see the details on the leaflet I've attached.

Will you come? It's important. Don't come for me. I also understand that there are more important things than tending to the body's needs, remember. Not many things, but there are some.

And who will stop me from doing both? Come, pretty monkey! I'm starving! And the meeting is important.

For Anna's sake, if you'd like to think of it like that and if it'll bring you to the meeting. And for Anna's future children. Yes – look at things that way. Come for Anna and the future.

But more importantly: for me – in the present!

Hurry, pretty monkey!

Lots of loving
   (not allowed to say 'love'!)
      Siwsan.

01/08/99: AM

One month since accepting their 'invitation' to the Sunset House; three weeks since the last time They made us write in our diaries.

Keep it up, $\Omega\Delta$!

At least the treatments have continued nonstop – and my body is reacting obediently to Their commands. There'll be a good harvest when the Sunset comes – The Day of Honour.

The treatments are relatively painless, but the effects are not. The first of the week is always the worst – but there's some sort of treatment like tablets or injections or assimilation rays every day.

The Rest – younger than us Sunseteers – do the work, with one or two of Them supervising. We're lucky, in a way – there aren't enough mature unhumans to put them to work somewhere like this – but I spotted one, some weeks ago, through my cell window, crossing the lawn.

Is there another member of The Few in the Sunset House, I wonder? Am I the only one on Lv.3? Yet Pedr managed to get a letter to me. How did he do it?

Every chance I get, I search closely for the sign that shows that one of The Rest is one of The Few. I thought I had found one yesterday, but the scar was a centimetre or two closer to the left ear than it should be.

I wonder if it was a mistake. Was that poor soul meant to be one of The Few? Misplacing a half-centimetre of platinum – denying any chance for his salvation. Such a thin line!

His salvation? Perhaps it's Pedr and I and The Few others who are lost, and The Rest – platinum-less, temptation-less, following the letter of the law – who are saved? Isn't the feeling – the guarantee – of becoming a part of the omnipresent, ageless and all-knowing the only meaning of being 'saved'? And today, aren't those in total accordance with the Computer-General the ones who fulfil those criteria? Aren't they the ones who have that 'pleasure'?

What would Aunt Bodo say, I wonder? About a computer – be it the Computer-General or not – being a god?

The Computer-General rules, governs, creates the new from the seeds of the dead, determines the dates of birth and death, the skin colour and even the mind's wanderings.

Is he not a god, Aunt Bodo?

I hear her answer: 'Man made the Machine'.

Well, what's the difference, Aunt Bodo?

And I hear her answering again – no, it's not Aunt Bodo answering, but Siwsan: 'The difference? I'll tell you the difference: love. A Machine cannot love.'

My dear Siwsan – what did you ever know about love? Loving, perhaps – you were so good! Did you know you put a smile on my face and send a shiver down my spine, even today, as an old man? And you – a what, I wonder?

What are you, Siwsan? Where are you, Siwsan? Turned to dust? One of The Rest by now, perhaps? Not one of Them – unless you are a part of one of Them. Or one of The Few, still? It's possible – you were smart enough, and had plenty of conviction.

What did you know about love, Siwsan? Now that I think about it, I think you did know all about love from the start, didn't you? Isn't the only meaning of love the act of loving? And what is the act of loving if not creating the most perfect unity possible?

And here we come back to the Computer-General, once again. Who could deny that the Computer-General has succeeded unequivocally in his mission? Hasn't the Computer-General, by endeavouring to create the perfect unity, manifested the perfect love? So, what's the difference, Aunt Bodo?

'Sacrifice', she would surely say.

Listen, Aunt: Cwansa, in all his glory, will be able to debate your answer: 'Sacrifice is an exchange; what's valuable becomes worthless in a way which is eventually recouped.' Isn't this what the Computer-General has done?

Who's next? How about Pedr: 'The Infinite and the Finite; that's the difference. A few electromagnetic messages – a bit more complicated than usual – and his finiteness would be exposed. No, the Computer-General isn't infinite; and he isn't God.'

Only you, reader from another age, can weigh and measure the truth in Pedr's words.

And Anna – what do you say, Anna? Anna says nothing, just stands there on the campus lawn, in the early-October sunshine, the beauty of the flowers rotting, eventually recouping what they lose.

You stood on this same lawn, didn't you? Three weeks ago. Here, through this window, in the July sun. On the lawn where a monstrosity walked, an instant before you appeared.

My imagination, of course! Pure imagination. No one told me how sometimes there's more truth to imagination than the senses.

Did you recoup what was lost in the end, Anna? What new fruits sprang from the dead, Anna? What is it you lost to be able to recoup?

See the result: the total ascension of the Council of Fraternities; the Computer-General is a god; The Few are the limp dregs of freedom, the remainder of humankind turned to free puppets. The abomination of the unhumans, the nightmare of the Sunset Houses and their ghastly storage basements.

Fifteen years ago, the fate of the world was in the hands of The Few. And the fate of The Few in the hands of one.

I don't believe in what I believe. I don't have the right to. There's no proof.

There's nobody on the lawn. No illusion nor abomination. There's no lawn, either – just plastic grass and the old man that I am. Mam is making blackcurrant jam and fixing my socks. She's wrapping the jampot in thick layers of old newspaper and packing the socks carefully in my suitcase, with love. She knows the Computer-General is not a god. She knows of Love, Sacrifice and the Infinite.

That is why she's making jam and sewing socks, saying nothing.

## Marc's Last Diary : 08

01/09/99: PM

What did I write before lunch? Lunch – well, that's one word for it!

It's okay for The Rest. And Them as well. The Rest are so completely assimilated that it takes them nearly an hour to eat their feast of five tablets – they slobber and savour every lick as if it were a mouthful of delicious food. Afterwards they expel gas both ends, pat their stomachs and wipe their mouths and the backs of their hands.

That was almost the only time I wanted to negate the platinum – so I, like The Rest, could savour those five tablets as well. It's hard for one to sacrifice so many feasts just for the pleasure of retaining some of one's individuality and identity – especially seeing as the assimilation is so strong, and the community pattern so alien.

The temptation is growing every day – the 'meals' are getting worse. This is most likely another example of $\Omega\Delta$'s increasing effect on the current system. The Rest, of course, haven't noticed the 'meals' getting worse – the assimilation works like a tasty sauce for them!

Today, there weren't any tablets, even. We got cattle feed pellets instead. Of course, they're very rich in protein – and also, honestly, the pellets are closer to food than the totally synthetic tablets. But it's hard to forget the daily marches from the halls while chewing the feed pellets.

These feed pellets are for cows, of course. So that They can have meat. I could laugh out loud! I might as well. It's such a surreal state of affairs. It's like a dream – everything is topsy-turvy, but still making some kind of sense within the framework of the dream.

Serving us cattle feed so They can have meat! Are there really any cattle? Where are they? Where are the lush grasslands, and where are the springs still silently flowing?

It's likely there are cattle somewhere – four-legged machines of flesh that go 'Moo' – in some sterile cowshed underground. Cattle which have never seen clover, nor whipped at midges with their dungy tails.

Those four legs are likely suspended from some plastic ceiling checkered blue and white so the meat on their legs gets tender; suspended with their heads tilted up so the pellets can slide down their throats more easily, and their manure can fall more cleanly. Possibly falling to lower ranks of cows, to become part of their feed.

I forgot to mention how the pellet feed would be healthier than the meat from creatures like those.

If They aren't hungering so much for meat, then why are they going through so much trouble to metamorphosise the Sunseteers as cattle before serving them up on a plate? Is this part of the acting and faking as well, like the plastic leaves that change colour?

Or does a sliver of respect for our fellow humans remain under Their metallic skin? Does a small part of that special and trivial absurdity (which was once part of human nature) still exist in Their being? Does it make Them aware of the extra-chemical difference between animal meat and human meat? If so, it wouldn't surprise me if They also go through the trouble of faking the curlews crying for rain, and the seagulls screeching above the shore, and the ripeness of blackberries ready for picking, full of juice (or maggots).

If that's the case with Them, then there's hope. From within.

## Marc's Last Diary : 09

01/08/99: Evening

By now I'm beginning to notice that things here are a little different to what I'd heard – both officially and unofficially – before accepting their 'invitation'.

Before coming here! When was that, pray tell? Only calendars have the right answer: just a month!

In some ways I was lucky before coming. As one of The Few, I had the platinum, which keeps giving life meaning. And hope, as little as it may be, gives that meaning a justification.

I was also lucky before the total de-humanisation. Pedr too, and a few others I recognised. Our training and experience had prepared us to undertake 'upper work', and for a time during the early years of the Council of Fraternities, and before the total de-humanisation, we enjoyed all the freedoms of the 'upper workers'.

Then the final choice, fifteen years ago. As one of the upper workers – one of the chosen few – I had to choose between registration and 'adaptation' to turn me into one of Them, or, along with the 'lower workers', complete assimilation – mentally, directly, irreversibly – to become one of The Rest.

Mine and Pedr's choice, as well as The Few others, was to accept total assimilation – putting our trust completely in the platinum wire, expertly placed. The initiative succeeded, to some degree. They never discovered the secret of the platinum, and they registered us all as assimilated beings just like The Rest, despite the platinum having negated the total assimilation of the brain.

Not for everyone. Many of The Few were lost because the platinum had been installed incorrectly; is it any wonder, given the mad rush? And the platinum wasn't the perfect defence for the rest of us.

The number and condition of The Few started to dwindle. We were ineffective as a single body. The whole thing was a failure. The remnants of The Few had given up any hope of being able to dethrone the Council of Fraternities. It was too late.

We hadn't noticed, so many years before the total assimilation and the de-humanising, how treacherous that assimilation was, how silent, subtle, indirect. We hadn't noticed, either, the importance of the early Council; I hadn't taken Cwansa seriously – but hadn't he lived under the same roof as us? And hadn't the corruption and perversion of the Council, and of Cwansa himself, become embedded so gradually that we all were blind to the danger?

Poor Cwansa! I feel for him so. But isn't this pity the result of what was lost due to his sound principles becoming a breeding ground for evil? Isn't the object of our most absolute pity the man who becomes a puppet, as wicked as the one who pulls the strings may be? There was no way anyone could have known, in the early days long ago, that poor Cwansa's small movement would become the seed of the most accursed of mankind's creations: the Council of Fraternities. There was no way anybody could have imagined the horrific results of the corruption and perversion, and the changing of hands early on.

And when the reign of the Council of Fraternities was witnessed worldwide, who would have thought back then, even, that total de-humanisation would be the Council's crowning achievement? That the inevitable installation of the Computer-General as dictator would be its result? And that 'purifying the environs' with the accursed assimilation rays would be the first electronic pearl of wisdom to come out of the mouth of that dictator?

The silent, subtle, indirect assimilation in the earliest era was the beginning of the horror. We realised this too late: the protestations were weak, the resistance weaker still. Bitterly was how we came to comprehend it. And from the slowness, the weakness and bitterness, the end of mankind was formed.

Few are left. The fruits of centuries shrunk to nothing. A handful of ineffective people are the last descendants of an entire evolutionary lineage. Living fossils who own freedom when freedom is no longer practical; who are able to choose when choice is no longer a possibility.

Fifteen years too late – or is it fifty?

Is it you or I, Anna, who is to blame? Two questions or one? And if it's two, isn't the answer to one the answer to the other?

I'll never know.

27/09/49

My first summer holidays are almost over. I'm looking forward to being back. Maybe back to Siwsan, if she ever comes back!

I only saw Anna properly twice over the holidays, then some half-dozen times with the rest at The Twb. We'll never understand each other. Christ, I'll be glad to be back!

I should have replied to Siwsan's letter over two months ago. It didn't feel very important then, with my holidays ahead of me, and Anna nearby.

But Anna wasn't so close, after all! A few more days and Siwsan (maybe) will be closer than ever. Better write her a short letter tonight, before the holiday's over. It'll be worth putting a bit of time aside to scribble a few words on paper; a preview of sorts!

Perhaps I should have gone down to see her during the holidays – to Cwansa's 'important' meeting. The First Summit of the Fraternal Peoples! Aren't we all intoxicated by titles! Cwansa is quite naïve to think he can unite the world's minorities to form a powerful majority; and that he, Cwansa, can save those minorities with his fraternity! It's time he grew up a little and realised that the fate of the world and its people doesn't lie in anyone's hands except the almighty beyond.

And anyway, the First Summit was way too far away for something so silly. Siwsan or not!

She most likely went to the meeting. I know Pedr didn't. I'll get the whole story from Siwsan, if she comes back – and if we have time to talk!

Anna did nothing but talk the last time I saw her on her own, minus the rest. Sometimes she looks like she's eager for my company. Then suddenly, she completely withdraws from me – except in words. Why, with the rest in The Twb, is she so very friendly with me? It's almost as if she shows some kind of verbal love towards me at those times.

And how, despite her inexplicable duality, am I still so smitten? Why did I feel so grateful when she told me and Pedr that her scholarship application was a success? And why did I feel so unbearably happy when she said she'd chosen to come to our university?

And above all, why didn't she ever tell me in The Winllan, by ourselves, instead of at The Twb in front of everyone else?

I'll never understand Anna.


*Continued: after dinner*
There's nothing funny in my diary. No laughter. Perhaps that's because there's no laughter in my life.

But I'm having plenty of fun, as far as I can tell. Especially with Pedr. I was about to write it down here, several times; but whenever it's time to gather my thoughts and commit them to paper, it comes across as silly and fake, and the humour starts coming across as hollow.

Pedr and I had fun at Joseff the barber's yesterday. Old Joseff at his best, and everyone in stitches! But again, it's not worth noting. Why is that?

There's no sign of God, either. That's a sign of good mental health, according to a book I read. It's hard to accept the book's argument, that the sign of poor mental health is an awareness of the simple choice: God or no God.

I went to chapel once during the holidays. I don't like the idea of catching up with the Almighty between cast-iron columns, in a building that tries to combine the simplicity of early barns with the brilliance of cathedrals. I went there with Mam and Aunt Bodo, on the weekend Aunt Bodo was here. Maybe that's why there's so little God in my diary – there's so much Aunt Bodo in my life. I wonder if that's why there's so little humour here too? No, that would be a lie. One of those two might not laugh very much, but the sadness that both share is a happy sort of sadness.

I don't know why I'm not able to appreciate humour – or at least, not think it's important enough to write down here. I don't have the philosophy (is that the word?) to interpret this problem. I wonder if there's some kind of fear here? A fear of the future, afraid of some age dawning where I read today's humour and am totally condemned?

Talking rubbish. Playing with words. Worthless, meaningless. A philosopher who hasn't begun philosophising yet.

It would be better if I went for a pint with Pedr, but I won't. Not here. Not because I'm a spoilsport, but out of respect for Mam, and her firm belief that God is teetotal. For some reason, I don't think Aunt Bodo's God is!

*Continued: before going to sleep*
Just finished writing a letter to Anna. Haven't seen her for days, despite going to The Twb every evening. Also wrote to Siwsan, did that first. Must protect the future! Also, maybe it's easier to convey 'like' in words than 'love'.

It's lonely here. Pedr's still fickle and everyone else is still childish. And Mam, of course.

It's just the sound of curlews right now.

*Letter from Anna 4.*

29/09/49

Dear Marc,

I didn't make it to The Twb for 6, like you asked in your letter. I went later (as soon as I could around 8 o'clock), but you weren't there. So this a quick note to let you know what happened. (I didn't like the idea of maybe seeing you away from home without clearing the air first; the days are passing so fast, we might not see each other before university begins.)

You wrote how you were looking forward to the new term, that you were glad that I was going to the same university, and you were eager for us to enjoy each other's company again. If we can't understand each other here, what hope do we have of understanding each other there?

You ask why I act so inexplicably. I can't answer your question because I don't understand it. What behaviour? What's so inexplicable?

I'm fond of your company, Marc – very fond. What do I do which disproves this? I don't understand your question. Yes, of course I enjoyed walking with you and chatting to the sounds of The Winllan. But obviously you weren't enjoying it, were you? What did I do wrong?

No, I wasn't deceiving you by chatting to you at The Twb. I don't understand why you'd say that at all. Had I not said a thing – talked to Pedr or Ioan or the rest, and ignored you – would that have made you happier?

We have to be honest with each other, Marc. I want to be honest with you. Yes, I was afraid in The Winllan, a little before I left, when you went to hold my hand. I know you won't believe this, but something like an electric shock went through my whole body, when you did something as simple as that. I got scared. Not of you, but myself.

I'm being honest, Marc – yes, I left The Winllan in a bit of a panic. I was escaping. But not from you – from myself. I wasn't afraid of myself in the café, in company. That's why I was behaving differently.

You let me down, Marc. You don't understand me. The me in the café was the real me – not in The Winllan. In The Winllan – not in The Twb – you saw a false version. One which came from fear.

I've been honest with you, Marc. Be fair to me in return.

I hope I can be with you in the new environment. Perhaps it's best we don't see each other in the old one anymore.


My best wishes,
   Anna.

15/10/49

If I'm sure of anything, it's that life is worth living. Finally, I get Anna, and she gets me.

I'll never forget the lawn in front of the University, Anna standing there. She was so different – so different to that Anna who ran away in The Winllan and then chattered nonstop in The Twb. So different from her last letter a fortnight ago – and yet, somehow, it explains her letter.

You'll never be a mystery to me again, Anna.

I feel sorry for Siwsan, but there's no room for both in my life. That's how it goes – and an agreement is an agreement. It's funny either way: I never thought I'd see the day when I'd rather Siwsan talk of love than loving.

Poor Siwsan! After all the fuss, and all the trouble getting back into University. But that's how it goes – and we did have fun.

I think I'll introduce her to Cwansa – they already know each other quite well.

Siwsan and Cwansa – honesty and knowhow; the free spirit and the constrained one; her laughter and his smile. Who knows what might come of such a match? Isn't the fraternity something they have in common?

What would Anna think of Cwansa, I wonder? Nothing bad would come of making introductions, now we've cleared the air. Not introducing her to Siwsan, of course! It'll be interesting to see how Anna reacts to Cwansa's lofty ideals and his little fraternity.

Cwansa's a madman these days. I lent him my copy of *Brave New World* a couple of days ago and he talks about it nonstop! I didn't really feel like reading it this time, but I remember it having quite an effect on me when I read it for the first time about a year ago. It's like a new Bible to Cwansa, from what I see, and it's fired him up to work harder than ever before (if that's possible!) to make his fraternity a powerful worldwide, anti-totalitarian movement. Cwansa, the poor man who dreams globally, while his family are stuck back in Africa.

I only see Pedr in lectures these days; he's left digs. Mari's to blame for that!

I should probably introduce Anna to Mari at some point. I'd rather not – Mari is sure to mention Siwsan. I can imagine the conversation! Suggestions, insinuations, nail biting; the polite laughter to convey indifference, as nails quietly dig into palms in protest. Piercing glares as smiles meet other smiles. Ych-a-fi – I could really do without that, to be honest!

Got a letter from Mam today. I need to answer her soon so she knows her visit on Saturday won't work for me. And a quick note to Aunt Bodo reminding her of my address. But it's way too late to write tonight. Second year work looking interesting and promising. What will these new discoveries bring about, I wonder?

Nos da, Anna!

## *Letter from Marc's Mother* 2.

13/10/49

My dear son,

I thought about waiting for a letter from you before writing, as we'd agreed, but seeing as such a long time has passed without a word from you, I thought it best to write a note in case something is wrong.

Is everything alright? How was the journey back? I'm sure the work is as hard as ever, which would explain how you never got a chance to write.

Remember to let me know if you need anything. I forgot to ask if you wanted to send your clothes home for me to wash this semester, like before. But it's likely you'll want to wash them over there this time, as you haven't sent a package this week. Remember it's no trouble at all to wash them; it also gives me the chance to fix a button or do some darning as needed. They most likely won't do that for you over there.

I had a chat with Pedr's mam yesterday. She hadn't heard a word from him either, so we thought it would be an excellent idea to call over there next Saturday to see you both. We won't stay long, of course – just a quick visit. Perhaps we could meet your new friends, see where you're staying and where you study. Both of us would love to see.

Pedr's mam had a chat with Anna's dad, and he understands that she's settling well, although missing home a bit. Very natural, of course. Do you see Anna from time to time? Most likely you don't, as she doesn't read the same subjects as you.

Aunt Bodo came the day before yesterday. I wasn't expecting

her to, but I was glad to see her still. She gave me a little present to pass on to you, but told me not to post it to you. Send her a letter if you get the chance. I can bring it to you next Saturday.

That's all until Saturday. We can chat about everything then.

Much love,
   Mam.

01/09/99: AM

Two months gone by. No other letter from Pedr – the first was most likely the last. No sign of any other members of The Few within these walls; nothing from nobody.

Two months. If life has taught me anything, it's that time – the time that's measured by the fragile stimuli of life – doesn't belong to the ticking clocks nor calendar pages. There's not much relation – is there any? – between those two times; clocks don't measure the length of ages, and calendars don't measure eras.

Two months in the Sunset House. A third of the 'holiday' is over. A third of the way until The Sunset. A third of the treatments before the harvest.

It's gone. The two remaining thirds will go the same way. That's one of the few things in common with our time and the time of clocks: they both disappear.

It's hard to tell whether these two months went slowly or quickly. The treatment, and the assimilation ray that makes it through the platinum, confuses all sense of time – both kinds.

We sleep half the time we see on the clock; sleep derived from drugs, not tiredness nor the desire to sleep. The 'resources' enrichen during sleep, and the treatments and our schedules were designed with this in mind.

Five hours of the day are spent eating twenty-five tablets: five tablets per meal, five meals a day. The assimilation, of course, turns the tablets into something to feast on by The Rest. No wonder why The Rest welcome their assimilation: wouldn't the assimilation be acceptable if it turns such measly sustenance into a feast?

After sleep and feasting, there are seven hours of clock-time remaining: two hours of 'treatment' and five hours free.

Free? What is freedom?

I see The Rest – the rest of Lv.3's residents – enjoying their five hours of freedom. Ninety-nine beings in the form of humans of both sexes; their bodies seventy years old, undergoing two months of treatment.

I won't go into details. If you are reading this, forgive me for not doing so. If there is any decency belonging to your age, reader, then you surely would not forgive me if I detailed their five hours of freedom.

Freedom? Their freedom is the freedom from all abnormalities; and normality to them is the perfect aping derived from their assimilation programmes.

Perhaps I and the other Few don't have any worldly freedom anymore. There came the ultimate end to that freedom fifteen years ago. But we still have some measure of the other freedom. What to do with that freedom?

And alas, we've only been mourning the bodies captured so far!

So, what is true freedom, reader? Do you have free time? And free brothers and sisters? Are you free? Do you possess freedom? If so, what will you do with it?

Consider your answer – and remember that you are human.

And we were once humans too.

# Part 2

**MARC'S MIDLIFE DIARY**
*05/01/1984 – 10/01/1984*
Alongside miscellaneous correspondences
from the same period.

– interspersed with –

**MARC'S LAST DIARY**
*01/09/99 – 31/12/1999*
Alongside an undated attachment from the
beginning of the twenty-first century

## *Marc's Midlife Diary* 1.

05/01/84

It's too late – for me, and the rest of The Few. There's no way to stop The Council. We missed our chance. It's all-consuming now. There is nothing we can do. Very soon, in a few days perhaps, they will begin the final phase, and we won't be able to stop it.

It's obvious that Cwansa is no longer one of us – in any way whatsoever. It's better to believe that than to believe he still doesn't know how far things have gone, and for how long. Anna knows deep down but doesn't want to admit it. Why didn't she tell him before it went too far?

Puppet or not, Cwansa's influence was still strong until very recently – and his line of work allowed him to exert it. Why didn't he act? Did he not realise he had to?

When should one cut the rot from the flesh? And then, how does one decide when's best to replace the knife with balm? Can one be overly forgiving? Can forgiveness turn into resentment? What then? Did we conflate forgiveness with cowardice, and were we aware of this or not? Were we afraid of the rot, the evil seed cast in our own flesh, and taking to it with a razor blade?

Is it possible to condemn, punish, and then forgive someone, all at once? The Almighty perhaps could, but not mankind. Not me, at least. If I condemn someone and call for their punishment, then I wouldn't be strong enough to forgive them as well. Not really – it would just be a shadow of forgiveness: bitter, empty, hypocritical. But I must learn to forgive Cwansa, stop condemning him and any attempt to punish him. Who am I to judge him, then deny him forgiveness?

But if that's the case with Cwansa, where love isn't clouding my senses ... how could I possibly do the same thing to Anna, and condemn her and call for her punishment?

I don't know the truth; there's no way I'll ever know whether they're guilty or not.

And if they both are, don't ask me to be judge, jury and executioner.

# Marc's Midlife Diary 2.

*06/01/84*

In the past, when *Nineteen Eighty-Four* was nothing more than the name of a great novel, who could have predicted how on the mark it would be?

Tried reading it again yesterday. Some parts were still laughable – yes, I had the invaluable pleasure of laughing again – as laughable and off the mark as last year's horoscope. And some parts were completely illogical – they come across as very naïve today.

But in essence it's so close to reality; only the details are lacking.

And *Brave New World*? Is that as close to today as yesterday was? Or closer, even? Won't the next few days – if their ultimate plan gets going – bring us into that 'Brave New World'?

It's too late to change the order of things. But perhaps there's still hope. Hope is so strong when it's at its weakest!

Hard to believe those mere mortals I became acquainted with half an age ago would be the seed of The Few who own the only key (if a key is what it is) to hope's door. The only ones who can change the destiny of the world – if it can be changed.

And hard to believe those few mortals sowed, from their love of the disenfranchised, the measly harvest this downtrodden world is reaping today.

It's almost impossible to believe it. Why us? And how did that little circle of friends, those mortal few, get sucked into this vortex? Why us? What were the factors or deeds; the fortune or destiny that decided this was the time and place where the fragile hope of a future was stolen due to a loose, unconscious, trivial connection to each other? And a connection to those who planted that damned seed?

Cwansa and his measly brotherhood. Yes, measly! Cwansa and his futile zeal and his whirlwind crusade for the disenfranchised of the world. Cwansa the 'messiah', who behind closed doors picks his nose and farts in the bath like everyone else, and who picks the food from between his teeth with the holy pages of The Brotherhood's pamphlets.

But today – puppet or not – he's the one with his finger on the button.

Pedr too. Hunting for blackberries and girls. Chitter-chattering and struggling to make any decision whatsoever. Dear, wishy-washy Pedr – Head Engineer of the Accounts Department of the Council of Fraternities. Who would ever have believed this at the time? And who, today, would ever have believed what's happened?

Siwsan – she's not a minor figure either. And there's Anna, of course … and me.

In the name of everything – how did it come to this? Which stars and planets aligned to cause this?

It's all a dream. There's no way this is real. Why us – the few mere mortals who were thrown together in some hidden corner of the world, years ago?

But it isn't a dream: we have the key – the only key. If it exists. And Cwansa, the arch-puppet, has his finger on the button. And between Cwansa and me there's Anna.

Anna stands between heaven and hell – if what I've heard is true. But I don't know for sure. Is it true or false?

Does anyone except Anna know?

## Letter from Pedr 2.

06/01/84

My dear friend,

We can't wait any longer. We have to decide. Very soon it'll be too late. You already know The Few are ready, and they're waiting for you. You're the only strong, direct and *feasible* link between us and Anna, and through Anna, Cwansa. And Cwansa's the only hope we have.

For the sake of the world – why won't you act?

What is Anna to you now? Are you blind? You know everything I said is true. Why won't you believe me? Aren't omens only obvious to the people willing to look out for them? You know about the new plans, and you know what will come of them. You know there's no turning back. Haven't you also had the platinum installed?

Act, Marc. Not just the future is in your hands, but the past as well. Will you erase the future as well as tarnish the past?

The Anna that exists today is not your Anna. This isn't the girl you loved. You have to believe me, Marc.

She's a means to an end. She isn't Anna anymore. Weren't you the same thing to her, after all?

One man – that's you, Marc – has the choice.

In the name of everything,
    Pedr.

01/09/99: PM

I'm sure I spotted one of The Few today at 'lunchtime'. The scar was in the right place – at least that's how it looked at arm's length. Is that how I got Pedr's letter?

I tried to give him a sign without drawing Their attention, but I failed. At least I never noticed any clear reaction on his part. There were two of Them present, of course, one very nearby; maybe that's why I never got a positive response.

It's still possible he's one of The Few. Wasn't his face still one of total loathing as he chewed on his pellet feed? What better sign is there that he's one of The Few? And he, like me, was a bit later than The Rest in reacting to the post-mealtime assimilation.

Who is he? Not one of the group from fifteen years ago. What was his job? He was obviously someone at one point, if the platinum scar was what I actually saw. But what difference does it make knowing who he was? Like me (and everyone else), he has no past, present nor future in this place.

But still, I'd like to know. I'd like to have a conversation with him.

A conversation! I haven't one of those for two months. Exchanging shibboleths doesn't count. And the conversations were (very!) rare in the fifteen years before ending up here. Perhaps once or twice a month, undercover, for a few minutes, with the odd clandestine letter to bridge the chasm.

What would we talk about if I got the chance to speak with him today? Our nains, most likely! Our roots and backgrounds; of the times when humans belonged to families before becoming numbers belonging to Fraternities. Weren't these things important before we came here? Rejoicing in our individuality and proving it by showing interest in the past and pride in our roots?

Then we'd talk of today, of $\Omega\Delta$, probably: what's the news, what hope is there? And the recent past: acceptance and rejection, missed opportunities, facing the unknown vs. ignorance of it. Perhaps we'd talk about Cwansa. And others, their lives and times. And the rumours.

I wonder if I'd be brave enough to ask about Anna? Surely he'd know something about her. Could I ask him that question? I could ask about Anna and hear him confirming what I always knew to be true; hear someone else admit that Anna was not to blame.

Are you still with us, Anna? Are you one of Them, or still one of The Few? Are you part of The Rest, or someone else, someone different? At one point I thought I understood you, recognised you. But no, I never understood you, Anna. I only loved you.

Maybe that's why I loved you – because I never understood you.

That's why I still love you, Anna. Because I know I will never understand you – whatever you did or didn't do; whatever you are or are not.

The chairman's final vote shouldn't have been condemned for being the wrong one. And didn't everyone else's vote also land us in this terrible situation?

And who knows whether this situation even affected you?

01/09/99: Evening

I can think more clearly than at the beginning of my 'break' at the Sunset House. The assimilation's definitely getting weaker.

How much is the Computer-General straining by now? How many sub-programmes have been transferred to be able to interpret $\Omega\Delta$'s messages? Will the Computer-General ever be overthrown? Will there be a world of people who stand for freedom once again? Not just free people, but people who stand for freedom. Isn't that a higher state than being free?

The only hope is outside this world: only $\Omega\Delta$ can bring salvation now. And if salvation comes, what then? What will the millions of assimilated do? And the unhuman abominations which are quickly taking over? Would we be free to 'retire' them for ceasing to be human?

Cattle feed! Why not? Weren't humans destroyed bodily long before, when the electricity hit our brains during the first assimilation? And Them: if They are still human, haven't they – like all humans – forfeited the right to salvation?

That just leaves The Few. The Few who rejected the 'honour' of joining Them, choosing to live among The Rest. But why – is it because we believed that only this choice could give meaning to the future and reason to the past? Why did we think preserving these two things was a good idea? What benefit is there in perpetuating this system of free beings – how it's been for centuries – whose freedom is the same freedom to violate, mutilate, hurt, insult and undermine each other? Would the Computer-General's perfect world not be better?

Aunt Bodo would have had the answer. But I do not.

I have no idea why I chose what I chose. No one truly knows one's reasons for choosing one thing over another. We choose with our heart – then try to rationalise it with our head. Our reasoning did not lead to the choice being made; it's strange how we then don't understand that choice. And it's strange how I never understood Anna. I don't even understand myself. I don't understand anybody. Nobody understands each other – nor themselves.

There's only love, without understanding; love, because there's no way to understand it. And in the Computer-General's perfect world, everything will be made understandable. There'll be no room for love. Maybe that's why I chose the imperfection of freedom: to preserve my right to love.

Is that why Anna chose to become one of Them? Because there was no love in her?

## *Letter from Pedr 3.*

Marc,

I wrote to you two days ago and no answer. You've done nothing. Why in the name of everything, don't you want us to meet?

We're still waiting for the word, or a sign – what's it to be? Anna, or everything that ever was and will be? You don't have a choice between whether you keep your hands clean or not – just how much blood you'll have on them.

Cwansa will carry out the plan – possibly without even knowing, himself. The only way is through Anna. Two people is not an expensive price to pay.

Only Cwansa is in the position to switch the Computer-General's latest programme. Anna's the only one able to get Cwansa to do it. You're the only one who can make Anna act. It's crystal clear! What's your reason for refusing to believe everything I've told you?

You know better than anyone what will happen if we don't do it. And you know there's only two days left.

I know you don't care about giving Cwansa up. But what right – and reason – do you have not to do the same with Anna? Isn't sacrifice just another word for duty at the end of the day? In the name of everything and everyone – yes, Anna too, if only you understood – do or say something!

You saw the experiments on animals. You saw the effects of the assimilation rays. I wonder – did you see the experiments on people? You wouldn't be holding back if you did.

And the 'adjustment'? Believe you me – the assimilation plan is diabolical, but the 'adjustment plan' is beyond the imagination of Satan himself. Only a machine could come up with such a plan.

We have two days. There are fewer than a hundred people who've had the platinum installed successfully. Obstructing the Computer-General is our only hope.

No – the choice is even simpler than that: surrender the figure that used to be Anna to preserve the qualities which once made her everyone's idol.

Marc, my dear friend – hurry! I have nothing to hide. You must believe me.

Pedr.

*09/01/84*

A very cold day. It was cold at The Institution despite the heating being on. Some failure in the environmental sub-computer perhaps. Hard to believe a computer can malfunction!

Couldn't see much through the window. There wouldn't be much to see no matter how nice the weather was. The residue of the poison – as weak as it may be by now, three years later – limits how many people there are out in the open. And then, of course, there's the curfew.

I went out for a few minutes – readings were too high to stay outside longer. But I didn't see a single bird. There are two a stone's throw from here, from what I can hear. I'd give the world to hear curlews.

Work at The Institution is more banal than ever. What isn't these days?

Today I officially saw the assimilation directive in full. Reading between the lines, it's obvious Pedr's description isn't wrong – but there's no official mention of the 'adjustment plan'.

A letter also came from Pedr today – too late, of course. Anna can't say anything, so why try? And Cwansa's too far gone to do anything. And how do we know Anna's in a position to be able to influence Cwansa? I'm not sure at all.

The computational regime is already too complex for us to do anything about it. Even if Cwansa wanted to act, there'd be no guarantee he'd stop it all. Haven't the computers all developed self-defence mechanisms by now?

And who even knows if Cwansa is Cwansa? People keep saying

how the initial phases of the 'adjustment plan' have already begun with some.

I should have gone to the last meeting. The Few are so weak now. Why didn't I go? Pedr's hiding something. He hasn't told me everything that happened in the last meeting yet. Is he afraid of hurting me? Or is it just fear?

Yes, a letter came from him today – but he knows my answer without me having to write it. Why can't I hear the full story of this last meeting without him hiding anything? Maybe then I would take action, if I had all the facts.

I have no right to compromise Anna without those facts. What if they're incorrect? Even if they were, I wouldn't sacrifice the living past for the (infinitesimally small) possibility of resurrecting the dead future. Because the future is dead. And the past, and Anna, are too valuable to sacrifice.

*Letter from Pedr 4.*

Marc,

It might be too late by the time you get this. It's such a joke, in this day and age, and in our line of work, that you're making me communicate with you in writing.

This is your last chance, Marc – unless it's too late. You've seen the latest programmes created by the Computer-General for The Rest. Do you believe me now?

I know you're refusing to act because you doubt the facts. I also know you think I've concealed the part of the report that deals with the last meeting – and Anna, of course. But believe me – it was all the truth.

But if you still think you shouldn't sacrifice Anna because you don't believe us, then ask yourself: wouldn't Anna's sacrifice be miniscule – she who's so perfect, if that's how you wish to think of her – compared to what will come of that sacrifice?

I discussed this with some of The Few nearby. They agree with everything I've been trying to tell you. Forget principles – what are principles worth in a world of machines incarnate?

You got the platinum, like I did. You know, as I do, that we're giving everything up to the computational regime. You had the platinum installed because you thought giving up wouldn't be the right thing to do. Do you still believe that?

Or are you – Lord have mercy on me: I never thought of this before! – are you more corrupt than Cwansa? Do you willingly want the freedom of the future to be limited to a select handful of people? Why? What plan – or conspiracy – is this?

God forgive me – you too. I don't believe my own opinion, Marc; I only beg of you. If you refuse to act, won't this opinion be the verdict of your future?

The future! Hear me laugh! There won't be a future if you refuse to give Anna up. The past it is, then. This will be the verdict of your past. And I believe you're placing more importance on that.

For the past's sake – act! Then again, maybe it'll be too late by the time you get this. Yes, it will be too late. May the past forgive you, Marc. I don't understand you.

There's nothing left to say. Nothing worth saying.

Pedr.

*Letter from Anna 5.*

Dearest Marc,

By the time you get this, it will of course be too late, but no matter. Weren't you too late years ago? In school, whenever you borrowed a pencil or a book or some other random thing? In The Winllan, as we ran from ourselves? In The Twb, drinking the coffee we obviously weren't enjoying? On the campus lawn? During the years in between?

I'm writing, despite all this, to thank you. You gave me so much. You gave everything except one thing, the one thing I desired more than anything: your love. You never understood me, Marc. Or if you did, then you didn't understand love.

You kept your love, the one thing I desired most, from me – then you cursed me with Cwansa's. Why did you ever introduce us? Why did you place that burden on me? Did you believe … no, it's not my place to try and understand you from your past actions.

I know you reject my explanation for what happened at the last Fraternity meeting. Be that as it may. You alone have the choice – to believe me or not. We'll never see each other again after today. At least, Marc and Anna won't.

Today is the end, Marc. The end of love, and so the end of everything. I only ever experienced love twice in my life: Cwansa's for me – and mine for you.

Anna.

# Marc's Midlife Diary 4.

10/01/84

It's over.

I chose an hour ago, along with the other Few. They still haven't found out about the platinum. No letter from Pedr – nor anyone else. Last words before.

They're here. I hear Them. No time. Hiding this.

We fight.

01/11/99: AM

Two months without writing in our diaries; and two months before the end of our 'break'. The treatments keep coming.

Where did the last fifteen years go? Fifteen years without hearing from Anna. Fifteen years of hell – a free man, in a living body, in a brightly lit pen.

It was hopeless, there weren't enough of us. A hundred, maybe? And the platinum was far from ideal. Fifteen years in a world imbued with the Spirit of Fraternity. And The Rest. And Them, the all-seeing ones. And the Computer-General, Man and Machine. And the unhuman abominations.

Was this what you'd dreamt of, Cwansa? And had you imagined this, Anna? How about you, Pedr?

One thing's kept me sane – my love for Anna. Although she never understood love, nor did she accept it.

It's hard writing today. The treatment, perhaps. That's how it is, sometimes. I'll be fine tomorrow. Up and down.

No letter from Pedr. No sign of the person I thought was one of The Few.

The assimilations are getting increasingly rare. But The Rest are so assimilated by now that blocking the assimilation rays won't have any beneficial effect on them.

It's likely that $\Omega\Delta$ is causing this inconsistency. Is there hope, I wonder?

That's enough for today. I'm old, and tired. I'm looking out the window – perhaps I'll see Anna standing on the lawn.

No – best not. Perhaps I'll see an abomination. I'd give the world for a blackberry jam sandwich, and to hear the curlews. And to see the little seagulls above the shore. And Anna. Lord, forgive me my incredulity!

01/11/99: PM

Fratolish hiang perpetshki

fratolish hiang perpetshki

fratolish hiang perpetshki

ubi-umgobo hiang perpetshki

ete-umgobo hiang perpetshki

hemi-umgobo hiang perpetshki

al computerex

al computerex

al computerex

fratolish hiang perpetshki

fratolish hiang perpetshki

fratolish hiang perpetshki

anak perpetshki

quanak perpetshki

computerex perpetshki

31/12/99: AM

I want to forget today's the morning of the last day. The Computer-General would like that. I'll also try to forget this afternoon, while writing in my diary. The Computer-General would like that too.

The Computer-General himself came to see us yesterday. The Man, of course, not the Machine. I think he came to take a look at us. I felt the Spirit of Fraternity everywhere. He looked rather fraternal when he arrived – like us, but also like a Machine. His eyes flashing, unseen by everyone else, like the flashing electronics of machines, with his elegant, metallic skin.

I touched his skin. It wasn't cold, nor metallic. I felt a jolt filtering from his body into mine.

The lawn and flowers are very pretty, thanks to the Computer-General. Anna was on the lawn. She was there yesterday too. So very pretty, and shy.

The bell.

The last lunch. Food. It's a tradition for the last lunch to be food. Must go, past the lawn. Lv.2 went past the lawn yesterday. To have food for lunch – and become food for lunch. To accept their honour.

Past the lawn, just over there.

Anna's still there.

*Marc:*
*in praise and condemnation;*
*forgiveness, persecution;*
*for honour and derision.*
*I write in love and hate*
*I knew, yet I never knew.*

# PARTHIAN TRANSLATIONS

## DEATH DRIVES AN AUDI

Kristian Bang Foss

Winner of the European Prize for Literature

———

£10.00

978-1-912681-32-7

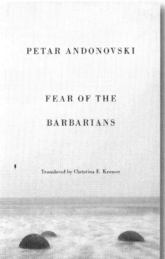

## FEAR OF BARBARIANS

Petar Adonovski

Winner of the European Prize for Literature

———

£9.00

978-1-913640-19-4

Creative Europe

# PARTHIAN TRANSLATIONS

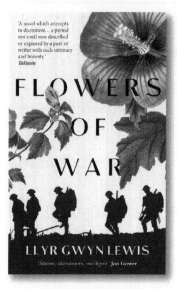

## FLOWERS OF WAR
Llyr Gwyn Lewis

Short-Listed for Wales
Book of the Year

———

978-1-912681-25-9
£9.00

Translated from Welsh by
Katie Gramich

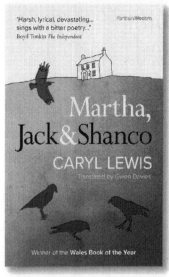

## MARTHA, JACK AND SHANCO
Caryl Lewis

Winner of Wales Book of
the Year

Translated from Welsh by

———

Gwen Davies

978-1-912681-77-8

£9.99

Creative Europe